A Family Portrait

Ray Hollar-Gregory

AUTHOR'S NOTE

This book is a work of fiction. Names, characters, places, and incidents are either the product of the author's imagination or are used fictitiously. Any resemblance to actual people, living or dead, business establishments, events, or locales is entirely coincidental.

Table of Contents

Introduction

Jordan Baros is an older man. More than two decades have passed since Jordan and Trina reconciled and began to live a more purposeful life, embodying the pleasures and challenges that come with it. His sons, Chad and Jared, are adults now, and Jordan is a grandfather to Jared's two children, Aisha and Sean. His sister, Wanda, and mother, Rachel, depend on his leadership and support. The pursuit, at this point, is family, not just for themselves, but for the affection, happiness, and legacy of all those they love and care for.

Chapter 1

Someone was knocking at the door, and the pounding resounded throughout the house. It was a heavy knock with no regard for the sweetness and sanctity of a home.

"Mr. Baros, are you in there? Open up. It's the police!"

Reacting to the urgency of the intrusion, Jordan gathered his pants, which were hanging on the bedpost, and headed shirtless downstairs toward the command coming from the other side of the front door. The dark silhouettes of two men were apparent through the shaded, beveled glass of the door because of the dim lighting in the foyer. Jordan opened the door in a state of curious uncertainty and surprise.

"Sir, are you Jordan Baros? Can we come in?" the voice of the stranger standing on the welcome mat commanded.

Jordan, still perplexed and anxious, replied, "Yes, can I ask what this is all about?"

"We need to ask you a few questions."

"Sure, of course. What is this regarding? How can I help you, officers? Has someone been hurt?"

The officers stepped into the foyer; the three men were now face to face. Jordan's mind searched for stability but found none. His only anchor was an initial thought that one of the cops was black, which might be favorable to him, but on reconsideration that seemed of no consequence. The invasion of privacy had no racial significance. The officers were dressed in sport coats with open dress shirts; the white officer had a dark shirt and tan trousers, and the other a pinstripe button-down with black pants and a gray blazer.

"My name is Detective Caggiano," the shorter of the two men with the Frank Sinatra swagger said, "and this is my partner, Detective Brown."

"Yes, can I help you?" Jordan responded, voice an octave higher than normal.

"We want to ask you a few questions. Is there somewhere we can sit, or would you prefer coming down to the station for questioning?" asked Detective Caggiano, again asserting his authority in spite of being in someone else's home.

"Questioning? About what?"

"As I said, we'll be asking the questions," Caggiano abruptly responded.

Jordan felt uncomfortable as he led the men to the adjoining dining room. The detectives surveyed the surroundings like two K-9 German shepherds as they followed him.

"You are a lawyer and worked with the prosecutor's office at one time, didn't you?" Detective Brown asked in a baritone bass that complimented his bulk although his chest and waistline were of the same dimensions; extra-large.

"Yes, about four years ago. Is this related to one of the cases I handled?"

"Wow, you won't quit with the questions, will ya? Fuckin' lawyers gonna cross examine everybody," Caggiano sarcastically remarked, shifting his eyes to look glancingly at his partner, Detective Brown. "Let me be clear—we are asking the questions here. You being a lawyer and all may want to cooperate with us so we can get this matter cleaned up without any difficulty. You know what I'm saying?" Detective Caggiano repeated a line he had habitually delivered over thirty years of police work.

Detective Brown added, as if on cue with the good cop, bad cop routine, "What my partner is trying to say, Mr. Baros, is that we want to make this as easy as possible for everyone. Do you know this woman?" He pulled from a manila envelope a photo and handed it to Jordan.

Jordan nervously held the photo but instantly recognized the woman in it. It was Toy. His mind began to sort the recall and attempt to connect the distinct events relating to her. The trauma of his time with her rushed through his body, like the feeling one experiences with a jet at liftoff until it reaches altitude. Toy, a girl he knew from the peep show in Times Square. It was one of the pictures from her portfolio that Jordan had seen when at her apartment. Looking closely and realizing there was no way he could deny knowing her, since he knew they knew, he looked up and answered, "Yes, I know her."

"How did you know Towana Simmons?"

Past tense with a solemn facial expression . . .what's up with that? Jordan thought. "I met her several months ago."

"So how would you describe the relationship?"

"Friendship. Look, I'm sure you guys know her background. She worked at a peep show in Times Square. I met her there—went out after that. I still don't understand what that has to do with anything."

"Towana was found murdered."

"Murdered! What happened? I'm sorry to hear that. But you know I had nothing to do with it." Jordan dismissed any remorse and skipped straight to self-preservation, realizing how serious the matter was.

"Mr. Baros, you are a person of interest in the murder investigation of one Towana Simmons because evidence has identified you as one of the last people to see her alive. We'll need you to grab some things and come down to the station house for questioning."

"Am I under arrest?"

"Yes, and let's make this as easy as possible." Detective Caggiano began to read Jordan his rights. "You have the right to remain silent. Anything you say may be held against you in a court of law. You have the right to an attorney. Should you not be able to afford one, the state will provide one. If you decide to answer questions now without a lawyer present, you have the right to stop answering at any time. Do you understand your rights as I've read them to you, Mr. Baros?"

"Yes, I understand, but on what grounds am I being arrested?"

"You are a prime suspect in the murder of Towana Simmons, and we need to get more information from you. We can place you at her apartment and in the area. We are awaiting the autopsy for the exact time and cause of death. Besides which we have an outstanding bench warrant for a parking ticket given to you on February twentieth, which coincidentally also places you in the area. We need to talk to you about a few things. Please stand and turn around; place your hands behind your back."

"You are arresting me for a parking ticket?" Jordan exclaimed as he placed his hands behind his back and did as he was told, mind in a haze, thoughts abounding. *How could this be? Get a grip. This will be cleared up,* he thought. "Can I put a shirt and shoes on?" Inconsequential acts in ordinary times that took on greater significance in this circumstance.

"No problem. And yes, we are arresting you for an outstanding bench warrant. You a lawyer, right? You think you're above the law?"

Jordan led the way up the stairs with the two officers

following closely behind. His nerves caused him to lose his balance and stumble on the steps.

"Be careful. You all right?"

"Yeah, I'm fine."

Inside the bedroom, Detective Caggiano undid the cuff on his right hand, leaving the handcuffs to dangle from his left. Jordan reached into the closet and grabbed a polo shirt. "I need to get a jacket from downstairs on the way out. And can I make a phone call? I need to call my wife and let her know what's happening."

Caggiano looked at Brown, who nodded affirmatively.

"Make it quick," Detective Caggiano said.

Jordan dialed Trina's work number and extension.

"Hello, Trina Baros speaking. Can I help you?"

"Honey, I need you to listen and not get upset. I need you to meet me at—" He turned to Detective Caggiano, who was standing right next to him.

"Jersey City Precinct 35 on Communipaw Avenue," the detective said.

"Who is that talking? What's going on?" Trina asked.

"I need you to meet me at the Jersey City police station on Communipaw Avenue in Jersey City. And contact Clifford Barnes. I'll need to speak to him."

"Jordan, what's happening? Are you in some type of trouble?"

"Yes, they are taking me into custody for a ticket and claim I know something about a murder."

"Murder? Are you kidding me? I don't have time for your sick humor."

"This is real, Trina. Call Cliff—you have his firm's number—and meet me there as soon as possible. I'll tell you everything when you get there."

"OK, I'll call him and meet you at Jersey City police station, where?

"Communipaw Avenue."

"OK, I'll be there."

"Please hurry. I'll see you later. Love you—bye."

"Let's go," Detective Caggiano said as he motioned to

Jordan to turn around for him to put the cuffs back on.

"Do we have to do this? The neighbors and all . . . it's such a spectacle."

"It's procedure, but I'll handcuff you from the front, and you can place your jacket or something to hide the cuffs."

Once inside the station house, Jordan was booked, photographed, and fingerprinted. The sergeant advised him that he would be held overnight to be arraigned in the morning and sent to the county jail.

"My wife and lawyer are headed down here. Will I be able to see them?"

"They're coming now?"

"Yes, I called before we left my house."

"Yeah, they can see you briefly, but the arraignment is tomorrow. They can appear in court with you then when they set bail, if the judge grants it."

"What is this, some third-world banana republic?" Jordan yelled.

"Calm down, Mr. Baros. Don't make me have to taser you," the officer casually responded.

Jordan was forcibly led away and placed in a solitary cell about eight feet by ten feet with a single cot, a white porcelain pedestal sink, and toilet.

* * *

"Jordan! Jordan! Wake up!" Trina said as she shook him from what appeared to be a terrifying nightmare. Startled and out of touch, he partially opened his eyes and gazed in bewilderment at Trina. "You were having a nightmare and talking crazy in your sleep again. What were you dreaming about this time?" Trina asked.

"Oh my God, it was so vivid," Jordan said, pushing the words out, still in a half-dream/half-reality state. His cognitive processes searched for stability. "I was reliving the time the police questioned me about that girl's murder in Jersey City. It's that same reoccurring anxiety I have. That situation years ago? Everything, it haunts me endlessly.... seemed so real, like an episode of Law and Order but worse. I was arrested, handcuffed, and about to be arraigned for murder. I guess this will haunt me for the rest of my life—the police, the suspicion, and that girl's murder."

Jordan had recurring flashbacks and nightmares, PTSD,

of that incident and related trauma during his period of addiction. Sometimes, during waking hours, he would feel anxious and have panic attacks. He was prescribed medication for anxiety by a psychiatrist, which he took on occasions to stem the attacks.

Trina moved closer, providing body-to-body contact to comfort Jordan, whose complexion was flushed. His body temperature was hot, and he had been sweating. "Honey, that was years ago. You have to let it go," Trina said in a soothing voice. Having dealt with his episodic traumas for years, she instinctively knew the necessary response to reduce the pressure and console him.

"Yeah, I know, but it still haunts me. Thankfully, it all worked out." If not for the rape kit evidence and DNA tests, Jordan might have faced the possibility of a homicide trial and life in prison.

"No more talk, you relax now, it's over. It's been over, baby. Take your medicine and relax. Go back to sleep," Trina said, having gone to the bathroom and gotten a glass of water and his medication, Xanax before going back to sleep.

* * *

As a young man in New York City in the 1980s, Jordan was self-indulgent and addicted to drugs and sex. His unabashed hedonism offered him the satisfaction he craved. The city provided the shadows to pursue his acts, similar to the internet, obscurity within an infinite public square. The bars, the bustling crowds, the restaurants provided a cacophony of social interaction with strangers. Jordan, as social media is inclined to do, felt empowered. But it also discourages intimacy through anonymity. The city also challenged Jordan's values and attitudes and was his demise. He had abandoned things that were now most precious to him. He descended into the dark web. The urbanity and its sophistication were completely indifferent to him as they were to everyone. The soiled existence led him to episodically share time with a sex worker/escort/hooker who introduced him to crack cocaine, addiction, and ultimately thoughts of suicide.

Upon reflection, it was not she who had made his choices. If it hadn't been her, it would have been someone or something else. In the end, the choices we make are our own, and until we account for our acts, the cycle continues. He ultimately went through rehab and had been drug free for over twenty-five years, but during his darkest hour, he became a suspect when the body of Towana Simmons was found abandoned in a vacant lot. Jordan was implicated when the police found his business card in her apartment and a parking ticket issued to him at her apartment's location.

Now, decades later, he saw life after the storm—a different space and time. For some, maturity and luck teach them of their insignificance in a vast unrelenting universe. The voices of aging speaks to those who are willing to listen. Aging means slowing down to appreciate what you previously failed to observe, decelerating, accepting, and knowing that wealth, materiality and self-aggrandizement count for little. Like the city or the internet's apathy and chaos, the wisdom can make you feel like a nobody. Ironically, it also strengthens you and helps you to find order in the chaos—it brings meaning and makes you feel genuinely alive.

Chapter 2

It was Professor Jordan Baros's last year before early retirement, and he had mixed emotions. He enjoyed teaching and serving as director of the Black Male Project. The project was an effort to retain and increase African American males' graduation rates. A dismally low 30 percent of entering freshmen graduated within a four-year period—considerably less than the 55 percent overall student population. He looked forward to other possibilities, still undefined. He told friends and colleagues that he wasn't retiring but "transitioning." He entered the classroom somewhat anxious with discernible butterflies, which were incomprehensible after all these years. As with an actor who goes onstage after years of performances, the adrenaline was the injection that moved the performance—a cup of Starbucks also helps.

The first day is equally anxious for the student and the teacher. As Jordan walked in, the students reflexively came to attention like recruits facing an army drill sergeant for the first time. Who is he? What is this class going to be like? His Rate My Professor comments say that he's a tough grader.

An invisible undertow consumed the tiered classroom. There were about thirty-five students in the room. Jordan scanned the audience and took attendance, apologizing in advance for mispronounced names. He instinctively took mental notes as he read the names, relying on generalities, stereotypes, intuition, and sensory perception to assess each student's potential. Slackers and achievers were easily distinguishable by body language, lack of eye contact, and responses to their names being called—unscientific and statistically flawed first impressions from an experienced educator. His processing was delayed a nanosecond by an eye-catching, attractive female student in the front row. The undetectable hesitation normally drew a smile or slight tilt of the head or comparative eye contact from the acknowledged, such as occurred in this instance. In addition, she flicked the flock of hair that shaded her left eye with her hand and crossed her legs. The student, if not the others, was conscious of the acknowledgement and responded as described. Life had blessed her, in its random pool of genes. Her facial features exhibited natural symmetry shrouded with dark hair that fell like silk drapes against an architecturally designed window. She was aware of her impact and had learned to use it to her advantage. She was of tender years but not innocent or naïve.

The first class was always procedural. Professor Baros, after handing out a syllabus and informing the students of its availability online, discussed the course requirements. He then presented a brief biographical sketch of his credentials and background. All eyes were riveted, and some students were taking notes until he broke the tension. Aware, from years of experience, of the natural tension of the first day, Jordan said to the class, "Relax. This is a marathon, not a sprint. We will be together for approximately fifteen weeks. As of today, everyone has an A; we will see who maintains that excellence over the course of the semester."

There was a slight crowd reaction and even some body movement to a more relaxed posture. He continued his remarks, "This is business management, and as business majors, it is a critical course in the development of your business acumen. You have, prior to this course, taken other, more general business courses. As second-year students, you will start to focus on more specific areas of business such as marketing, finance, human resources, et cetera. This course's subject matter will be mastered through initiative and effort. For example, no matter how much I were to study, trust me, I would fail quantum physics. That is not the case with this course. You can master this subject as long as you commit the necessary effort." There was some snickering by the students. "Are there any questions?" Professor Baros asked the class.

No hands raised, nor did anyone initiate a question. Professor Baros continued his lecture by talking about his philosophy as an educator. "I expect and will hold all of you responsible for the assignments including exams, homework, online reading, class participation, and attendance. If you hand in an assignment late, even if it is an excellent work product, it will be marked down by two grades. Is that fair?"

After a brief moment, the attractive student in the front of the class broke the reticent quiet and said, "Yes, I think it's more than fair, professor."

"Why is that, Ms.—what is your name?"

"Sonya Chambers," the student assertively responded.

"Why is that fair, Ms. Chambers? Isn't an A an A?

"Yes, it is, and you can give me an A if you like." The rest of the class chuckled at her response. And one can imagine how some admired her aggressive confidence in this new environment, headed by this older, distinguished, and naturally intimidating man.

"Well, I won't, and I can't. Again, I ask, why is it fair?"

Ms. Chambers responded, "I assume part of our education is meeting the requirements in a timely manner, and it isn't fair for those who have applied themselves in a responsible way to have their efforts measured the same as one who is less responsible."

"Very good, Ms. Chambers. I changed my mind; you get an A for the course," he said, and they both smiled. "Unfortunately, I can't do that, but you are exactly right. I am a different type of teacher, not just academics, reading, and memorizing for purposes of taking an exam. I am going to build your character and evaluate you on your progress.

"I believe it's a major part of my responsibility to prepare you for life outside the classroom. I think one of the most important determinants of success is conscientiousness. I reject the theory that the difference between success and failure is 'so-called' intelligence. So, don't come and tell me that you aren't as smart as so-and-so; therefore, your grades are lower. It is your effort and perseverance toward a goal that will distinguish the A from D or F. Am I right?" Professor Baros asked as he pointed to a student in the back of the class.

"Yeah, I guess," the student replied, as if he was unsure of what was happening and preferred that the professor leave him alone. Professor Baros automatically placed him in the slacker column.

"Look, I am not your typical academician; I didn't spend most of my career studying business management or other esoteric business principles and theories. Prior to teaching, I spent the bulk of my career in business as an executive and corporate attorney. Throughout the semester, I will share my experiences with you in order to transform the textbook material into the reality of the business world. I will mold and teach you how to be business leaders. I hope to change your perspective and appreciation of the game of business for a successful future career and life."

Professor Baros again paused for a moment, contemplating what he had just said and gauging the students' reaction to him—he was pleased. The butterflies had long passed. He paced in front of the room, stroking his mixed gray beard exemplifying a reflective, thoughtful sage.

"How many of you have an Apple phone or another Apple gadget?" he asked the class. The majority of hands shot up. "I guess the rest of you are Samsung users. That's OK, I'm not a hater. I have both, to tell the truth, I have an iPhone and a Samsung notebook, and I personally prefer the Android operating system to iOS. But here's my point: How many of you own Apple stock?" No hands went up. He continued, "I own about a thousand shares of Apple, not to brag, but what would you prefer to own: a thousand shares or the phone, iPad, watch, or whatever else you have?"

He could see from their faces that he had triggered a thought and awakened a dormant consciousness. Collectively, the students—like a church congregation during a minister's sermon—murmured to themselves, each moved by the energy of the thought Professor Baros had planted. Had this been a Baptist church, someone would have shouted, 'Amen.'

"So, I want y'all to keep buying those Apple products because every time you do, my stock portfolio goes up."

Professor Baros continued his preaching, telling his charges about the differences between a consumer and a businessperson. Imploring them to start thinking like a businessperson. "Money, wealth generation, and appreciation—not consumption—should guide your decisions and control your impulses. As future leaders and heads of families, and as y'all say, 'Be Woke,' become aware, stay informed. Don't think that the good life is a job and a check every two weeks. Invest in assets that will grow over time. Buy real estate, stocks, and bonds; start your own business; own the casino, don't just play in it. These are the things we will explore this semester, and I look forward to the journey we will experience together."

The new generation of students, the so-called "millennials," had access to a wealth of information that Professor Baros hoped to transform into knowledge. "I had to use an encyclopedia, something none of you are aware of. You guys ask Siri or Alexa and can tap a vast canyon of current and updated information. Use it to make a difference; convert information into knowledge."

Professor Baros wrapped up by saying, "This is not going to be a passive experience for you. So, if you're hoping to sit back while I entertain you, this is the wrong class. Sorry to break it to you, but you're going to have to think and think critically. I will be calling on you and your classmates, and we will debate the issues and hopefully come to a better appreciation of the things we are studying."

He answered a smattering of questions about the textbook and types of exams that would take place over the semester. He ended by assigning the first chapter for the next class.

As he was collecting his materials to leave, he looked up and noticed that Ms. Chambers had lingered behind the other students and was standing next to her desk. "That was an excellent response to my question. Most students don't get what I'm saying about responsibility and accountability," he said to her.

"Maybe because 'responsible' has always been something I've had to be. I am the oldest in my family with a younger brother and sister and, recently, a son. I was raised by a single mom. Everybody relies on me a lot. It comes natural."

"You make it sound like a negative thing."

"Oh no. I love my family, and they love me, but

sometimes things are hard. School, work, and family takes a toll." There was a youthful determination in her eyes and soft voice.

"I understand. Let me know during the semester if there's anything I can do to ease the load."

"Thank you, professor. I am really looking forward to this class."

"This is just the beginning; we have a long way to go. I'll see you Wednesday," Jordan said as Sonya was walking toward the door to leave.

Looking over her shoulder she delicately responded, "OK, bye bye." Sonya left the room knowing she had made multiple impressions on her professor.

Chapter 3

Jordan and his wife Trina lived a rather private life—
venturing delicately into the social spotlight and retreating
to the security of selves. They had many acquaintances but
few genuine friendships and were most comfortable
dedicating time and energy to themselves and their
immediate family. They were friendly and outgoing when
engaged but had no compulsion to be socially steroidal.
They had clear personality distinctions. Each wondered out
loud on occasion how they'd survived for so long—the yin
and yang of years of marriage and five-year prior
relationship. Jordan was secure and confident, socially
adept and humorous. Trina was more cautious and
reserved. She saw life as a black-and-white proposition,
literal and serious. Jordan accepted the lightness of being
and the existential randomness of it all. He had more
friends on social media than Trina, if such a stat is a
measure of sociability. Always engaging, but sometimes
you wouldn't hear from him for months to years; however,

when you made contact, it was as if you had just spoken the day before. Trina was more guarded—genuine friendships were few and limited. Loyalty was her main criteria for friendship. In contrast, Jordan looked at the glass as half-full, and Trina pessimistically saw it as half-empty. Both were unpretentious, self-assured and genuine.

Over time, Jordan had developed a que sera attitude, and if there was a flaw in his character, it was his directness, and quick wit which could be interpreted as narcissist and sarcasm. He would ask Trina, on occasion, if he had unwittingly insulted or intimidated someone during a social conversation. Trina would respond that he had. He was oblivious and at the same time sensitive to most social cues; he was empathetic if not obviously so. Their differences were also what had attracted them to one another. Despite their personality differences, they were synchronized when it came to the certain things.

Both were fiercely committed to the best interests of their family, which included their two sons, Jared and Chad, and two grandchildren. Jordan's past transgressions, ironically, brought them closer together. He needed Trina's stability, and she needed his risk-taking, factors that served their union and balanced their common perspective. Trina's impulse control combined with Jordan's romantic ventures brewed a sweeter blend than either could have made on their own. It is uncanny how the differences between them made them each a better person.

* * *

Recently, during the early fall, Jordan and Trina had invited a couple they had known for years to spend a long weekend at their country home in central Virginia, just outside Charlottesville. They'd spent the better part of the first day there together touring the natural beauty of the Blue Ridge Mountains and the charm of historic Charlottesville. Its rich cultural, natural, and artistic history was showcased in a selection of colonial museums, galleries, shops, and parks that were dispersed throughout the area. The many beautiful parks, rivers, and lakes offered the perfect setting for sports, picnics, relaxation, and adventure. The couples had also visited charming boutiques, antique shops, antiquarian bookstores, and distinguished local wineries. Around midday, they had brunch at a quaint eatery that served the best chicken and waffles outside of Roscoe's in LA. It was nearing dusk when they completed their excursion with a tour and tasting at one of the area's finest wineries. Later that evening, the couples returned home to relax and converse over the bottles of wine they had purchased.

Marcia and Bill, were an interesting pair. Marcia was Trina's friend; they'd met while working on a voter registration drive one summer about ten years ago. Marcia was Trina's opposite. She was an extreme extrovert with thousands, if not hundreds of thousands, of Facebook friends and Twitter followers. She was a former state assemblywoman and at one time was approached to run for lieutenant governor of New Jersey. Bill, on the other hand, was less public and had spent his professional life as a certified financial planner advising high-net-worth clients. Together, they had done well; they were an urbane, well-traveled power couple.

Jordan was indulging in his second glass of cabernet sauvignon reserve, as was Bill, when he asked, "So, Bill, what should I do about this market and my upcoming retirement? You can give me some ideas, right?"

"You know it's going to cost you."

"Negro, please, you drinking all my liquor and eating my food—what's happening with the stock market? You know I'm deep in the market, and I've done well over the years, but I remember too many times when the market has gone down, and that shit sinks. It goes down faster than it goes up. You know I can't get caught in one of those downturns at this age. If the ship goes down, I'll have to move in with you and Marcia. You've got about six or seven bedrooms."

"Man, if that market tumbles like it did in 2000 or '08, we are all up shit creek. Look, I tell my older—sorry, man, I mean mature—clients, you gotta diversify. Mix it up, and even keep up to twenty-five percent in cash. If the market goes down or we go into a recession, none of us are safe. The game becomes—or the winner is—whoever loses the least."

"I'm younger than, you so don't start with that old stuff," Jordan said.

"What? Two months, you crazy." Bill laughed as he said it.

"What about annuities? Does that give me the protection I need at this point?"

"I don't like annuities, and as I said, mix it up, but don't put all your income into annuities. The thing with annuities is yes, you get a lifetime of income—guaranteed periodic payments for as long as you live. And y'all—well, at least

Trina—will live a long and happy life, so the risk of that hits the insurance company cause they agreed to pay as long as you live; they would prefer if you die early. Bill hesitated and sipped his wine before continuing. "But since you and Trina both have defined benefit pensions, they'll pay until you die, and your social security is an annuity as well."

"What do you mean, Trina's gonna live a long life? Man, don't get it twisted. My chronological age ain't got nothing to do with my physical and emotional age. I'm about forty emotionally and physically."

"Yeah, all right, man," Bill said dismissively. "As I was saying, if we can get back to seriousness and not the wine talking, we can ask Trina about your physical ability. But, back to the matter at hand, you can tailor the annuity to do a lot of things like inflation protection and predictability, but it will cost you, and, if you ask me, the insurance companies are the biggest winners with these products."

Just then, Trina and Marcia entered the room, having been on the front wraparound porch talking and enjoying the background melody of nature's critters while drinking vodka cocktails Trina had concocted. "What are you two talking about? No business. This is a day of peace and relaxation," Marcia said.

"That reminds me," Trina said as she turned to Marcia. "We need to schedule a spa day at this fabulous wellness spa up here."

"That sounds good. We should take our men. Do you want to come, Bill?" Marcia chuckled as she asked her husband.

"What? I'm not going unless Jordan goes. I can't leave my boy. I do need a massage; that would be good."

"Well, Jordan?" Trina asked, looking in her husband's direction.

"I'll go, but just a massage—not all that other stuff. I don't want to spend the whole day there." Time being of the essence to Jordan, spas, manicures, and massages did not rank high on his list of necessaries.

"Like you got so much to do," Trina said.

"OK, just the massage, no facial, hot oils, or all those lotions. I feel like a greased perfumed pig after I leave."

Looking at Marcia, Trina said, "The man is so common."

Jordan looked at her side eye without a verbal response. He quickly dismissed the comment facially and returned to Bill. "OK, what are the cons for annuities you were talking about before we were rudely interrupted."

Trina paid no attention to Jordan's shade and moved to sit closer to Marcia, away from their husbands, to renew their chat. Out of nowhere, after everyone moved on to the next thought, Jordan yelled, "We can't go. I got a tee time tomorrow morning; we're playing golf. I forgot." Trina and Marcia both frowned, shook their heads in ridicule, and thought, Men are from Mars and women from Venus.

Jordan repeated his prior question to Bill: "What are the downsides to annuities?"

Bill snickered at everything that had just transpired and said, "Man, you are too much. Look, here's the deal," he continued. "You are going to get a lower return from the annuity than other asset investments like the stock market. Rates are low and fees, even the hidden ones, are high. There's a lot of fine print. The other thing is you lose control over your hard-earned money. Once you purchase an annuity, your capital is tied up in the annuity, so you never have access to the lump sum."

"A lot of my friends put their money into annuities for guaranteed security, but I hear you," Jordan stated.

"As I said, you got annuities with y'all's pension and social security. Take the rest of your retirement savings—IRAs, 401k, and 403b—and hold on, diversify, pull out what you need, be conservative, preserve, and you'll be fine. You got real estate, savings, social security, and pensions. You got all three—I mean, four—legs of the stool. You're good man. Just don't spend it all in your first year."

Before Bill could finish his sentence and Jordan could ask another money question, Marcia stood up, repositioned herself, and stood between the men like a referee telling two fighters to break, "Are you two finished counting your money? I want to ask Jordan something."

"Let me get some more grapes. You want some?" Jordan said to Bill as he stood and walked toward the kitchen.

"Yeah, I'll need some. This feels like we're getting ready to get into some heavy stuff," he responded. Trina also moved to the couch, and they were all assembled in a semicircle.

"I was watching this show," Marcia began. "Should I wait for Jordan?"

"I hear you," Jordan yelled from the kitchen, "Go ahead."

"What show?" Bill said.

"It was on Oprah's channel. Comes on Sunday mornings—Soul Sunday."

"I watch that," Trina said.

"Well, she was chatting with this author. Her name is Malia Chocrah—Indian woman, she writes about relationships, happiness, the universe. Her book—I forget the title; you can google it—talks about the three levels of love."

Jordan returned and poured wine into everyone's tilted glass. Marcia stopped talking, waiting for him to finish and join the conversation, "Go ahead, I hear you. There are three levels of love," Jordan said as a prompt for Marcia to continue.

"OK," Marcia began. "What is the level of lust and desire between you and Trina?"

"Watch yourself, man; you know she's setting a trap," Bill said.

"I got this, ten out of ten," Jordan responded with a boyish smile.

"You lying." Marcia said, as Bill and Jordan laughed. Marcia continued, "There is no way your lust is that high after twenty years."

Trina interjected. "Thirty-one and yes, Marcia, he's lying."

"What about you and Bill? You've been married for how long?" Trina asked Marcia.

"Eighteen years going on a hundred."

"You love it, baby. I am the best thing that happened to you," Bill said.

With an air of sarcasm, Marcia said, "Yes, dear, thank God. I don't know what would have happened to me if you hadn't saved me from myself. Yes, over time, we have made some adjustments. Bill has always complained that I don't love him as much as he does me, that I am in love with my career and before that, the kids."

Everyone sat forward at this juncture waiting for Marcia to continue each trying to anticipate where she was headed.

"It's been difficult. I was a dutiful wife, had the babies, officer in PTA, Jack and Jill and all, started networking, taking leadership positions, meeting people, and finally becoming a political junkie and running for the school board and getting elected. It seemed that I was outside myself, an out-of-body experience. There was me, little Marcia, mother, Bill's wife and then there was this other person, state representative, community leader, committee chairperson, speeches, applause. You can lose yourself and the things that are most important as you try to juggle it all."

"That must have been difficult for you guys," Trina said.

"It was. You know, we separated for a while; this was before we met you two."

"Girl don't get into it. We had our time. I told you about what we went through."

Jordan had been silent, taking it all in. "I think most couples go through the different stages, and we did. I have to give credit to Trina; she was the one who fought for us. She showed me true love."

Trina felt a flutter. "Oh, that's sweet." She puckered her lips at Jordan.

"All right, you love birds, back to what I was saying. Initially, we are driven by lust, control, and power, Chocrah says. The need to be right is a powerful force that stymies relationships. We argue over the most insignificant things. The struggle to dominate and control the other is due to the individual's personal lacking and need to overcome personal inadequacies."

"What do you mean? I don't argue with Trina because of my lack of self or to control her. I argue because she does stupid shit," Jordan remarked, only two seconds after having complimented her.

"OK, Mr. Genius, who bought a timeshare in Mexico next to the town where El Chapo's drug cartel lived? We can't even go there or sell it! Might as well have bought one on the south side of Chicago or Detroit. It would have been cheaper." Everyone laughed except Jordan.

"You got jokes, and it wasn't near El Chapo."

"You two stop, but it's exactly what Chocrah was saying."

"All right, Marcia, what is the bottom line? Where is this going? What is the higher level of love and relationship, if not the beginning? What is the end?" Bill asked.

"Sweetie, you know the answer; you tell me."

"Oh no. You started this; quit playing. You watched the show, not me."

"Calm down, Bill. The idea is that we try to move away from feeling the need to dominate, have control and power over others, and begin the natural process of love, which is intimacy without fear, no secrets. Accept each other's strengths and limitations without condition."

"I agree with that," Trina interjects.

Marcia finishes her thought, "You reach a stage that is mutually respected without the tensions of having to prove yourself time and time again. You can, in a solid loving relationship, overcome the need to own and dominate; you understand intuitively that the purpose of love is greater than self. Therefore, time is spent on more important things than quibbling over the insignificant. The control of the marriage adopts a purpose that it previously didn't have."

"OK, Marcia, that's nice in the abstract, but real talk—Trina and I talked the other night over dinner, and I asked her if she was happy she married me. She hesitated, so it wasn't automatic."

"I said yes," Trina stated.

"Yeah, she finally said yes. I think my dinner was cold by the time she did. But the point is, how much is one person responsible for another's happiness? I take the position that neither I nor Trina, or anyone, for that matter, should be held responsible for another's happiness."

"I don't understand. You're married to Trina; you both are committed to each other, but you say you're not responsible for her happiness?" Marcia asked.

"No, it's not that callous. Yes, we are committed in our marriage to a joint life, and that commitment is huge. Family values, raising kids—now grandkids—security, and comfort while respecting our individual differences are essential to true happiness."

"What do you think about that, Trina?" Marcia asked.

"I agree. I used to think that my sorrows, depressions, or if things didn't turn out the way I wanted . . . somehow

Jordan was responsible, and, trust me, Jordan has caused me a ton of heartache, but I have come to understand his flaws and mine. I will say this, though: there came a point when I took control and responsibility for the things I could. I stopped looking to Jordan for everything. I empowered myself," Trina said, leaning forward in a commanding posture and voice while still seated.

"So y'all don't look to each other for happiness?" Marcia asked.

"Our happiness is a result of our commitment to what I said earlier. We are happiest when our kids come over for family dinners, birthdays, and holidays or to celebrate their achievements in sports, career, education—that is the happiness we embrace. As two individuals, we have our own pursuits that also bring us happiness. Trina's career and personal friendships as well as other needs are necessary for her happiness and well-being, all of which I support and encourage," Jordan stated.

"I think that's what I was saying—that higher level— and you guys seem to be there whether you know it or not. This organic thing that is beyond what people think love and marriage are because of what the movies or media say they are," Marcia said.

"I'll toast to that. Let me fill our glasses," Jordan said.

The conversation eventually trailed off and moved to less intellectual things like reality TV, politics, sports and pop culture "Have you seen the last Atlanta housewives episode? The Kardashians? What about Trump?" Et cetera.

Later the evening, lying in bed before turning out the lights, Trina and Jordan reflected on the earlier conversation.

"We have come a long way," Jordan said.

"Yes, we have. Sometimes it's hard to imagine how much we have accomplished together in spite of it all."

"Yeah, life is a constant test, and we've dealt with those challenges, fell down many times and managed to get back up. I love you."

"I love you, too, honey."

Jordan cut the light on his night table. They pulled the covers up and held each other as they kissed softly under the quilt. Trina turned over and moved closer to where she could feel him against her lower back. They eventually fell asleep with his arm wrapped around her waist.

Chapter 4

Jordan had a budget line for a research assistant. He went through the state university policy process and posted the position on the university's employment website. He sincerely needed assistance to accomplish the projects he had scheduled. In addition, and undeniable, engaging with Sonya Chambers was also part of the motivation. Whether he acknowledged it or not thoughts of her personal presence outside of the classroom was unescapable. Shortly after the posting, he asked Sonya to see him after class.

"So how is it going? You seem to enjoy the class."

"Yes, I like it."

"Good for you. Hope I'm not too aggressive during lectures."

"No, not to me, but you embarrass—intimidate—some students."

"They deserve it," Jordan said contemptuously. "Did you hear Maranda trying to argue the gay rights movement is more significant than the sixties' civil rights movement?"

"Yeah, I heard that. I just thought, 'This girl ain't real.'"

"Same here, but did you notice by the end she said they were of the same significance. No. Still wrong. Race discrimination versus sexual orientation discrimination— for the most part it's a ridiculous argument. Any form of discrimination is intolerable, and if you happen to be in the group that's being discriminated against, you will argue that it's the most significant. I guess an objective analysis based on some statistical measure could determine which of the two has a higher value proposition in the progressive movement. I imagine stoners who want to legalize marijuana will argue that legalizing cannabis is the most significant movement in the last hundred years."

"You are too funny, professor. I agree she was a bit too personal and emotional—so subjective when making her point. She really came out today. I didn't know she was gay. Good for her."

"The feminist movement, the Holocaust, slavery—the list goes on; the inhumanity and victimization are endless.

In any event, it was a good discussion. The reason I asked you to stay after class is because I wanted to let you know that I'm looking for a research assistant to finish up an article for publication and to prepare for a conference I'm presenting later this year."

"That's good. You'll be able to do all those things you mentioned in class." She wasn't comprehending the application of all this to her.

"If you are interested, submit your resume, and it will be looked at favorably."

"I'm honored, professor," Sonya said, slightly blushing at the offer. "I'll do that. May I ask the pay? Hours?"

"Everything is posted online, you'll see. It's around twenty dollars an hour. Won't make you rich, but I assume you can use some extra money. Hours are flexible. We can work around your schedule."

"Thanks, professor. I'll look into it tonight."

"Any questions, you can ask me. Take my cell, call me. Anytime."

They exchanged numbers, and Sonya said, "OK, thanks. I'll see you tomorrow. I mean, next class; I get confused."

She started to leave and then twirled around to face Jordan, slightly tilted her head to the side gave him a faint smile while backpedaling and waving a gentle goodbye with her hand slightly raised.

Chapter 5

Jordan and Wanda's mom, Rachel, was well into her late eighties, and her health was deteriorating. Her physical limitations were becoming more acute. She was afflicted with multiple comorbid ailments including diabetes, hypertension, and early-onset Alzheimer's. The previous year, Rachel was hospitalized because of a mild stroke that affected her right side, requiring her to walk with a cane and receive home care rehabilitation. There was a regimen of pills and insulin injections she was required to take daily. Wanda had remarked to Jordan on occasion, *'Just managing the pills and insulin is a full-time job.'* The bulk of the caregiving fell on Wanda. Invariably, it seemed the case that the care and nurturing, whether of children or of elderly parents, tended to fall inordinately on women, whether daughters, sisters, relatives, or good Samaritans.

Jordan did his part with things more associated with

financial need and stand-in acts when Wanda needed him to take their mother to doctor appointments or pick up medicine from the pharmacy or just plain needed time to herself.

Wanda was feeling trapped and depressed, not just because of the demands of caregiving but also because of her mother's dementia and failing memory. Wanda cherished the memories she shared with her mom; they were the treasures accumulated over a life like a patchwork quilt of love, relations, good times, and those not so good— a life together. Those memories were the immutable bond that, at this stage of their lives, were to be mutually reminisced over and cherished. And now, those treasures would eventually be solely possessed by Wanda as they were fading from Rachel's grasp.

Besides the emotional and mental strains of elder care, Wanda often reflectively questioned her life in general. She was independent, not so much from wants but from need. She applied herself to her career and doused the flames of passion for finding love after a series of failed relationships. Those relationships included an affair with a married man, the pain of which still stung. Online dating proved to be unfulfilling, and casual sex became depressing and tiring.

Now in her forties, the likelihood and hope of a romantic relationship was not an issue that occupied her time; however, it did occupy her mind and left her heart hollow. In spite of it all, she was not devoid of the need. The subconscious was always present if not obvious. Uninvited, it pierced at the most inopportune times and, like a steel sword, could wound the spirit, body, and soul. Family events, holidays, weddings, watching romantic comedies, or even seeing couples holding hands could trigger the desire and the agonizing feeling of being alone and unloved. Wanda reflexively suppressed the longing, like a medication that soothed the symptoms but failed to cure the illness.

She was an unquestionably attractive woman who drew the attention of men—particularly younger men—when out and about. Since she had never had a child, her waistline, perky breasts, and rounded hips maintained a tautness characteristic of a younger woman. Her above-average height and confident strut distinguished her from the crowd. She was also a warm and pleasant person with a soothing temperament, admirable personal values, and loyalty that solidified friendships and caused them to be more than transient.

One such friendship was with a man named Romeo Hedics. Romeo was an attractive biracial gay man. Romeo claimed to have been heterosexual at one point, even married a girl in his twenties, which they both quickly realized was a bad idea. He did it to please his family, particularly his father, who had never accepted Romeo's sexuality. Romeo was four years younger than Wanda, and at one time, Wanda was his babysitter. They were from the same neighborhood. Romeo had attended Columbia, the same college as Wanda. Wanda was a senior pursuing a degree in communications studies while Romeo was a freshman majoring in computer science. She stuck by him when he "came out," so Romeo felt forever indebted to her for her willingness to listen and be supportive. Romeo was an only child, and Wanda was like a big sister to him.

They met this particular afternoon for lunch at a charming vegan cafe and juice bar that overlooked the Manhattan skyline on the New Jersey side of the Hudson River. It offered outdoor seating under an umbrella along a widened sidewalk. Wanda arrived first and was escorted to a seat and handed a menu while she waited for Romeo's arrival.

Rehana, the owner, approached Wanda, smiling and gesturing with extended arms for a hug, "So nice to see you, Wanda. It's been a while," she said. Wanda returned the gesture by standing up to warmly embrace her. Rehana had been influential in Wanda's interest in and transition to veganism. Pleasant with doe-like eyes and olive skin, she was of Mediterranean descent. Her alto voice and calm demeanor projected a spiritual balance of mind and body—Zenlike. There was a natural aura that was disarming to those in her presence—it projected a genuine universal connection and peaceful consciousness. Her presence was in accord with the plant-based vegan dishes on her menu. "Are you eating alone?" Rehana asked.

"Oh no. My friend Romeo is meeting me. You remember him?"

"Of course, yes, he's from Brooklyn, and I think the last time you were here, he was with you, right?"

"Yes, you have such a good memory," Wanda complimented.

"Thank you, you are so gracious, and you look beautiful as always." Always working the room Rehana said," I have to make my rounds, but I'll make sure the hostess tells you about our specials, and I'll check on you after Romeo arrives."

"Oh boy, everything is always so delightful; I think the specials will just confuse me. I have a taste for the linguine," Wanda jokingly responded.

Rehana bowed with hands clasped as she retreated and moved along to greet other guests.

Shortly after Rehana's departure, Romeo arrived. "Hey, baby girl," he said excitedly, loudly enough to attract not just Wanda's attention, but that of the patrons sitting outside.

"Hi, baby," Wanda responded in a more subdued but just as delighted tone.

"What's happening, girl?" Romeo asked as he took his seat under the yellow-and-white-striped umbrella that shielded the sunlight and noticeably matched his yellow plaid UNTUCKit shirt, beige khakis, and tan loafers.

"Don't get me started; you know it's never ending, and I don't know where to begin."

"Girl, please. Whatever it is, I know you got it under control. You always do. You know I tell everyone that you're my Olivia Pope. So, talk to me. What's up?" he said as he leaned back in his chair and picked up the menu.

"Ha! I wish," she said as she found herself letting out a belly laugh. "I really don't want to talk about it yet—not right now anyway. Tell me about you. What's new in your life, and who is this new boo you got plastered all over your Facebook and the 'Gram? I saw your posts, and it's not like you to be so public with your relationships."

"I am bitten, honey, and it ain't really public; it's just visible to my friends, but all you need to worry about is being happy for me."

"I feel you, but still, I don't think I've ever seen you post anyone other than yourself," she said unable to stop herself from laughing. "And baby boy, you know I am happy for you. I was just shocked to see those posts because you were always so secretive in the past. You two were all up in the Bahamas, partying at Lola's in the Vineyard—all over each other, all over the place."

"You only live once, and for too long, I've been hiding and sheltering myself based on what I thought others would say. Fuck what others think; their judgments are just a reflection on them. I am a free and proud gay man. Let the world rejoice or choose not to, but I decided that I'm not going to keep myself small anymore by worrying about what other people will think or say because I don't give a damn anymore."

"Preach! Yes, it's true. Hurt people love to hurt other people. I'm so happy for you, Romeo."

"That's why I love you. You have always been my sis. I could always come to you, without fear of judgment or ridicule. So, come on, as much as I love talking about me, tell me, what's going on? Have you taken a new lover?" he asked sarcastically.

"No, you li'l punk," she said laughing.

Before Wanda could elaborate, the waitress approached and introduced herself. "Hello, my name is Niki, and I'll be your server this afternoon. Can I start you off with some drinks?"

"Hi, Niki," Wanda said. "I'll have a glass of chardonnay and water with lemon." Romeo responded with the same response but a glass of merlot.

"I think we're ready to order," Wanda interjected, looking at Romeo for agreement who was glancing at the menu. He nodded affirmatively.

"We do have a few specials you might be interested in," Niki offered.

"Yes, that sounds good, even though I know what I want," Wanda said.

Niki smiled and began to recite the specials: "We have parsnip cappelletti, a savory whipped parsnip and crushed potato ravioli, shitake mushrooms with truffle oils. Also available is our black-eyed pea cakes, crispy cakes of Yukon gold potatoes, black-eyed peas, and chipotle aioli. Finally, you may want to try our Hziki seaweed Cape Cod cakes with tofu and vegan tartar sauce.

Wanda looked at Romeo. "You know what you want?"

"Yeah, everything, but I'll try the black-eyed pea cakes. Sounds interesting."

"Good choice," Niki added.

"You know, I'm going to stick with the menu and have the ravioli with cashew cream. That's filled with spinach and mushrooms?"

"Yes, and it does have pine nuts and a smoked tempeh,"

Niki added.

"I don't know what that is, but it sounds good and healthy, thank you."

"OK, I'll put that in, and it should be out shortly, I'll collect the menus, get your drinks and bring your meals when they are ready. Thank you," Niki said as she gathered the menus and left to place their orders.

"I can taste those pea cakes already," Romeo said.

"I'm starved," Wanda said. "But back to our discussion. There's nothing new to report in the dick department. It's been a while since I dated, and you know my last relationship was over a year ago. Remember that guy I met on that app, Blender?

There is a momentary pause and Romeo says, "Yeah, I remember, actor guy?"

"Yes, that's him. I created my profile, and we matched and texted for a while. He didn't ask for a nude, no sexting crap, so I figured he wasn't a creep like the others, and we eventually went out. It was good—we had fun. You know the actor types, life is a plaything, live in the moment, he had some credits, younger than me by seven years, but that wasn't an issue. After a few dates—dinner, movies, drinks at bars, the usual—it just stopped. I called him just to ask what's up, but he never returned my calls. Went ghost on me."

"Did you sleep with him?"

"Yeah, it was good. I was ready, but maybe I gave it up too soon?"

"When?"

"After the second time we went out."

"I don't know what to tell you. If you do or don't, who knows? If it felt right, there isn't a rule. Girl, you can't just sulk; you have to pick yourself up and stay in the game. You are a darling. Don't fret over these relationships. It ain't about you or them—it's a moment in time."

"Well, I guess my time is over," Wanda said.

Niki appeared and briefly interrupted their conversation, looking at both Romeo and Wanda, without saying a word she placed the waters and glasses of wines on the table.

Once Niki had finished, Romeo picked up his glass by the stem and gestured to Wanda to touch glasses which they did to a pleasant chime before he continued, "Shut up. Quit all this self-pity—it's not like you. Look, I have this friend I want you to meet. If he wasn't straight, I'd be all over it, if you know what I mean. He's a little older, late fifties, gray around the temples, nice body structure, still some lift in his ass. You know I checked that out."

Reacting to his comment about 'lift in his ass,' Wanda frowned her brow and shook her head.

"I'm going to have some folks over in a few weeks for a cocktail sip, a little get-together; you should come, and I can introduce you. We don't have to tell him. This is between me and you. Let's see what happens."

"You sure he's straight? Don't get me into one of those down-low situations.," Wanda said.

"Honey trust me. He's straight. He was married for years to a gorgeous but a little crazy Puerto Rican chick; they never had kids. She just proved too much. He's to himself—dates occasionally, but looking for something more, I think. You'd be good for him."

"OK. I'll come. Whether we hit it off or not, I always have a good time at your parties."

"Now that's what I'm talking about. That's the attitude I love to see and know. So, what else has got you down? How's your mom?"

"She's doing better since the stroke—alive if not kicking at eighty-eight years old—but caring for her is getting to be a bit much and taking its toll."

Just about that moment, Niki returned to the table with their lunch orders and placed the simmering plates in front of each. They both ingested the combined aromas, and Romeo unconsciously sighed, "Mmm."

"Can I get you anything more?" Niki said after the settings were in place.

"No, this looks delicious," Wanda responded.

After a brief moment of silence as they both tasted their food, Romeo continued their previous discussion by asking Wanda, "What about Jordan? Isn't he helping?"

"Jordan does his share, but less than me regarding her personal care. He helps out whenever I ask and when he can. I don't blame him. He has other responsibilities—his wife, my nephews the grandkids. He handles the financial matters, bills, and support Mom may need. We both do."

"Sounds like a lot is expected of both of you. I know this is a tough time. It's amazing how the parents become the children, and the children become the parents. Emotionally, I assume you're dealing with the guilt or stress of whether you're doing the best you can for her?" Romeo was insightful, and he often sympathized with Wanda. They'd had conversations about this in the past and similar talks with other friends.

"Yes, that's true, but I'm struggling with the idea of having to place her in assisted living or another senior care facility. I've tried to avoid it, but it is getting to be too much for me. She is so vulnerable, and I'm a big part of so much in her life at this time. So many questions, conflicted emotions, and no right answers."

"You have to accept the inevitable and realize that it's not your fault. You didn't cause your mom's illness or aging. Whether you continue to provide her care or seek professional help, her condition will remain the same. Plus, safety and comfort are things you may not be able to provide the way a trained caregiver can."

"Thanks, Romeo. This is helpful. I appreciate you listening and the advice. I don't know where to turn, and I feel therapy is ringing the doorbell. I have to talk to Jordan, and we'll have to decide how to handle things."

"Honey, hush. I'm sure y'all will work it out. And don't thank me for being a friend. We temporarily share space in this universe, and it's more powerful than either of us. Friendship and togetherness allow us to attempt to tackle some of this shit. Seriously though, begin to let go—not literally, but do the best you can, and don't be so hard on yourself. And make sure you come to my party, be among friends, and let me introduce you to some people."

"I'll definitely be there, and thanks again for the talk."

They finished their lunch and even shared a flourless chocolate cake. It was some two hours later when Romeo said, "Got to run, sugar. I'll call you with details during the week, and make sure you dress with some flair. Don't come stepping out lookin' like a librarian."

"Shut up, fool. I know how to pull it together. And that is literal—pull it together. Spanxs and tape are much more effective than the gym."

"You shut up. You're still the same weight since school."

"It's not the weight, honey; it's where it resides."

They both laughed and shared parting hugs and kisses. Wanda made sure to thank Rehana for the delightful lunch before leaving. It felt good being together that afternoon as she and Romeo departed to continue their separate lives in a better mood than before they met.

Chapter 6

A couple of weeks after Wanda's meeting with Romeo, Jordan pulled into the parking lot of his mother Rachel's apartment complex. He noticed Wanda's car as he was parking. He hadn't seen Wanda in weeks, although they frequently spoke by phone or texted each other. He was glad she was there and looked forward to spending the afternoon with his mother and sister. The siblings had grown closer over the last few years. There had been an incident that frayed their relationship years ago; although time had healed the wounds, it still occupied their subconscious. Wanda had told Trina that Jordan was having an affair. The disclosure caused a series of events that ultimately led to a separation and Jordan's personal decline. The unintended consequence was the intervention necessary to save their marriage and his life. Jordan had since come to realize that. At the moment one accepted personal accountability for their actions and stopped blaming others, rational thought and rehabilitation leading to redemption could begin. The linkage was tenuous, and he had never directly expressed his thanks to his sister for what she did, but over time, the silent expressions of his fondness and love for her had spoken volumes. They loved each other and cherished the comfort of their familial bond.

He walked up to the front porch, rang the chime bell, and awaited answer by either Rachel or Wanda. His mother opened the door with glee in her eyes and a complimentary smile on her face. Like the beauty of a bird in flight against a cloudless blue sky, her glow elicited a joy of the heart from Jordan. She instinctively grabbed his hand and pulled him over the threshold, hugged him, and stroked his back. The gesture and scent of his mother triggered a return to youthful security. The maternal warmth conveyed a soothing flashback to when he was young and needed her assurances that no matter how cruel the world, goodness was always on the horizon.

"My son, my son. Come on in and sit down so we can talk. I'm gonna make some grilled cheese; you hungry?" Before he could answer, Rachel said, "Your sister is in the other room on the phone. You know how she is always talking to somebody. That phone is attached to her ear."

"Yes, I'll have something to eat, but don't go to any

extreme. Just stopped by to see you and saw Wanda's car. I haven't seen her in a while."

"Wanda! Your brother's here," Rachel yelled as she turned to go back to the kitchen. Jordan retired to the TV room.

Wanda appeared shortly after, exhibiting a partial smile. She greeted Jordan with a hug and squeeze. "How you been, ol' man?"

"Tryin' to make it. How you doin'?"

"Just talked to my editor. They changed the deadline for this story I'm coproducing about black women's influence on the Black Lives Matter movement, and it stresses me that I've got to revise and cut critical pieces because of their arbitrary demands."

"Damn, it's too bad they don't appreciate your brilliance. Plus, creativity can't be time managed. I'm sure you'll get it done, and it will be great."

"We'll see. I have a meeting with production next week. And thanks for the compliment, even if you were being sarcastic," Wanda smiled.

Rachel had moved into the kitchen, and since her

hearing was limited, she didn't realize that Wanda had already entered the family room as she called for her to get off the phone for a second time. She was startled when she reentered to check on Jordan and bring him a glass of iced tea and saw Wanda was sitting in the room, "Oh my God, I didn't hear you come in," Rachel said. "I'm fixing some lunch for Jordan; do you want some?"

"Yes, Ma, I can do with some home cooking. All I eat is takeout and at restaurants."

"It's just some grilled cheese and soup. Nothing fancy. It'll jus' be a minute. You two relax, and then we can eat."

"OK, Ma, take your time," they both replied.

"I need to talk to Jordan about some things while you cook," Wanda added.

Rachel went to the kitchen to resume her preparations as Wanda moved closer to Jordan on the couch and, crossing her legs in a lotus pose in her Lululemon outfit, faced him within about three feet. "This is like old times—just me, you, and Ma," Wanda said.

"Well, almost. There was Tom. Dad." (Wanda and Jordan were half brother and sister.)

"I miss Dad," Wanda said.

"Yeah, I had my issues with him—everyone did—but he was the man I looked up to. He was my father. We had such a structured childhood; remember we always ate at five o'clock sharp? You had to be home no matter what."

"Oh yeah, then the dishes. Dishwashers didn't exist back then—at least, we didn't have one. And if you went back out, you had to be home when the streetlights came on," Wanda added.

"My kids didn't have the same experience. Sometimes, I don't know if it was good or bad. Only on weekends—and even then, not always—would we eat together, and most times it was at a restaurant. Trina can cook—it was one of the things that attracted me—but her various jobs and interests limited that. During the week, we grabbed TV stands after we got our food, and we'd eat in front of the TV."

"Yes indeed, things have changed; I miss those times— the spirit, togetherness, and conversation at dinner. Remember Thursday was always spaghetti with that Ragu sauce Mom made with hot sausage? That was the best. To this day, no matter where I eat pasta, that Ragu sauce and

Calandra's Italian bread are imprinted on my brain," Wanda said.

"Yeah, no question, same here. Then on Fridays, Tom would fry porgies with that Crisco grease and save the grease in a tin can for the following week."

"Talk about unhealthy eating. I can't believe it. You know I'm leaning toward veganism? It is a gradual process. I am trying to eat healthier. Although I'm not 'all in' because I do make exceptions from time to time, I am health conscious and have completely eliminated red meat and poultry from my diet, and that alone has me feeling like a new woman. I have more energy and am sleeping better. I mostly eat plant-based whole foods and watch my sodium and sugar. I must confess, though; I don't think I can ever give up my seafood. You know sushi is my biggest weakness. I guess you can call me vegan with an asterisk. How's your health? You mentioned some problems last time we spoke."

"My sugar is high. I was peeing every hour and not able to get a good night's sleep, so I got checked out, had a full physical, and now I'm on medication for type two diabetes and have to watch my sugar. You know how I love pastries, so I cheat sometimes. So that's it. Oh yeah, I joined the Y recently and go about three days a week. So basically, I'm watching my diet, exercising, playing golf, and medication. My doctor doesn't think I need insulin, so keeping fingers crossed and trying to manage. Getting old is not fun."

"It's better than the alternative. Diabetes runs in the family; I have no indications yet, thank God. Talking about getting old, what are we going to do about Mom?" Wanda continued in a lower voice. "You know Ma is getting older, and with her aging came the physical and mental ailments that we've both seen since her last stroke. I was telling a friend that I don't know how long I can manage to assist her by myself."

"I know, and I apologize. I know everyone expects so much from you, and my efforts haven't been as considerable as yours. It's my guilt and avoidance of reality. You know how controlling I can be, and when something is beyond my control, I avoid it. It's like some kind of defense thing. I'll do some research and talk to friends who've had to place their parents in assisted living. And don't hesitate to ask or tell me when you need help. I promise to do more. My work schedule will change shortly, and I will be more available. Have you spoken to Ma about this? What are her feelings?"

"Thanks, and I know you're there for us, I appreciate all you do. You know Ma; she thinks she can handle things and isn't really aware of her limits or maybe doesn't want to acknowledge them. She's always been independent. She has to use the walker if we go out to the mall or get something to eat. I'm not saying immediately, but we have to think about the future—the near future."

"I hear you, and you're right; we have to plan ahead. I'll look into it and see what I come up with, and we can plan together."

"What are y'all whispering 'bout in there?" Rachel shouted from the kitchen.

"I thought she had a problem with her hearing," Jordan remarked.

"Nothing, Ma. You need some help?" Wanda shouted back, rolling her eyes.

"I'm almost finished. Go ahead and set the table and come get the iced tea for us to share."

Turning to Jordan as she got up to head into the kitchen to help their mother, Wanda said, "We'll talk more. I have something else I want to share with you."

"OK, why the suspense?" Jordan responded as he picked up the remote to change the channel on the TV.

"Nothing. We'll talk over lunch. I want Mom to hear."

"OK, cool."

* * *

Jordan had already taken a bite out of his sandwich as Wanda was pouring the iced tea. "Let me say grace before you eat the whole sandwich," Rachel scolded Jordan. Saying nothing, he set his sandwich down on the porcelain plate as Rachel bowed her head to bless the food by thanking God for the meal before them. She finished with an amen. Jordan and Wanda chimed in as well.

"Now you can eat," she said as she looked at him.

"So, tell me, how are my grandbabies?"

"Everybody's fine. Jared works twenty-four hours a day. Aisha and Sean are growing up fast. Aisha's in kindergarten, and Sean's walking and getting into everything."

"Jared was by last week with the kids. He said Juanita was working. They spent the afternoon with me. Those babies are so cute. I never hear from Chad."

"I talked to him on the phone a few weeks ago. He says he's writing, working on his book. He talks to his mother. I pray for that boy. Ever since he was little, he was the strange one. I am here for him and have always been, but he doesn't open up, so it is hard to connect most times. I love him and want the best for him. We'll see," Jordan stated.

"Leave Chad alone. He's just trying to find himself. These kids have it a lot tougher than we did, with college loans and no jobs available. You got an education, found a job, saved money, got married, and, if you were lucky, bought a home and lived happily ever after. Well, at least some of us," Wanda said.

"I wish it were that easy, but you are right; the guarantees and security aren't as good as they used to be," Jordan said.

"How's Trina? I had lunch with her last week, and she just seemed distracted. I've never seen her so absent," Wanda asked.

"What do you mean?" Jordan responded.

"Hard to explain. It seemed like she had a lot on her mind and couldn't concentrate on what we were talking about."

"You know she has always been scattered—attention challenged. That's her personality," Jordan said.

"No, this was different."

"She is getting older. I've been noticing changes, and it's kinda scaring me—forgetfulness, keys, cell phone. Doesn't want to go out. I don't know why but she ordered the five-season DVD set of I Love Lucy, claiming that she loved Lucy when she was a child. I said, 'But you're an adult now.'"

"I don't know what that is, but I noticed something I hadn't seen before and couldn't ignore it. I hope she's all right," Wanda said.

"Some days things are fine, but other times I get concerned. Most people wouldn't notice the changes—too subtle—but when you've lived with someone as long as we have, they can be dramatic. I don't normally think about it, but I was looking at her the other day, and it startled me. It wasn't that I saw an older woman, but I saw myself, our mortality, and asked where the time went."

"You are scaring me," Wanda said.

"I can't believe you two. I'm eighty-eight. You children got so much life ahead of you. Wait till you get my age."

"I know, Mom, and hopefully we're that lucky," Jordan said. Wanda smiled and reached to squeeze her mother's hand.

"Well, let me lighten the mood. I have some good news to share," Wanda began. "I have decided to adopt a baby and have already started the adoption process."

"Oh wow! I am so happy for you," Jordan exclaimed while Rachel reached across the table, reciprocating the squeeze her daughter had earlier extended.

"When did you decide to do this?" Jordan asked.

"Well, I've been thinking 'bout it for years, and now is the right time, so I'm going to do it. I've been working with this nonprofit community organization in South Africa and traveling there for years. I met people and visited some orphanages. A good friend who's a social worker counseled me and helped with the paperwork. I'm just waiting for my baby; I'm hoping for a girl. I've researched South African adoption procedures, and I've been told the baby will most likely be of mixed heritage."

"What is 'mixed' in South Africa?" Jordan asked.

"It's a fairly diverse population. There's white Afrikaner, who are predominantly descendants of Dutch, German, French Huguenots, English, and other European settlers. There's a large Asian population, including Chinese and Indian, and a colored mixed race of people. The largest, of course, is the African or black, but it's not culturally homogeneous. They include Zulu, Xhosa, and other African nationals. So, we'll see. I'm excited."

"You are Ms. South Africa; you've always been intrigued by SA."

"It's all from my experiences from studying there while in college. I just fell in love with the country, its people, and the fight for human rights."

"We are excited for you," Jordan said.

"I told another friend of mine about what I was doing, and she questioned why I would adopt a South African baby when so many black kids here need a parent. I thought about it, and this is an emotional decision. I'm a humanitarian—a globalist. My attitude may be different from some others. I have a real kinship with Africa. I told her it's not an intellectual debate or a right-or-wrong thing; it's my decision. I have options and decided Africa works for me. Plus, you know, I've always said I intend, at some point, to live there. It's all good."

"Well, we support you, don't we, Mom?" Jordan asked.

"Of course. I can't wait to hold my African grandbaby."

Wanda and Jordan helped their mother clear the table and clean up. They spent a few more hours reminiscing while watching TV until they decided it was time to leave and gathered their things. Rachel had already begun to miss them.

Chapter 7

A few weeks after their lunch at the vegan restaurant Wanda left her place in New Jersey and headed to Brooklyn Heights for Romeo's party. She was dressed like she was heading to a club, rocking a rainbow fitted sequin jacket over a soft black cotton top and black tailored pants with matching heels. The thought of meeting someone, as Romeo had promised, was on her mind but not a priority. Too many blind dates, online dates, The Bachelor do-I-get-a-rose experiences in the past had jaded her. There was a natural resistance to setting oneself up for a letdown. Lowered expectations were a better approach and a defense against disappointment.

Romeo lived in the Brooklyn Heights Historic District. He owned a two-bedroom, one-bath co-op with a dazzling lower Manhattan view. She had visited his apartment before and considered moving to Brooklyn at one time. The place was contemporary and clearly reflected Romeo's colorful personality. It was posh with a sunken living room and a handicap ramp leading to beautifully varnished eucalyptus wood floors. The kitchen was small, but the minimalist interior design kept it from looking cluttered. You could gaze out from the kitchen onto a private terrace that had unobstructed views over brownstones, gardens, and the Manhattan Skyline. He had this amazing high-tech bathroom with a Jacuzzi bath, double-sink vanity, radiant heated floor, and large glass-enclosed steam shower. The Japanese TOTO toilet was artificially intelligent with a temperature-controlled seat, deodorizer, and warm water sprays. The last time Wanda visited, she used the toilet and nearly fell asleep. The spacious bedroom had a sixty-five-inch mounted TV along with built-in shelving that provided additional storage. Nothing in the apartment was more eye catching than the views of the Statue of Liberty and Lower Manhattan the moment you walked in.

Wanda was the first to arrive, about two hours before the party was to start. Romeo had asked her to come early to help with preparations. He was a perfectionist and a control freak. He was not easy to work with. Over the years, Wanda had learned how to deal with his madness and idiosyncrasies. Ignoring him seemed to be the best approach. Romeo became more persnickety and things became more stressful as it got closer to the start time of the party. On one particular occasion, Wanda had witnessed a complete meltdown by Romeo after a caterer forgot the calamari that he wanted for a taste-testing game he'd concocted for his guests. Romeo, with tears in his eyes, had retreated to the luxurious bathroom and closed the door. He refused to come out until the caterer was finally able to retrieve the lost calamari. Romeo's tantrum finally ended—it seemed like hours later.

"Wanda, I need you to fold the napkins and place them on the right end of the dining table next to the silverware. The food is simple—finger foods like hors d'oeuvres, shrimp, a variety of tapas and fruit slices, crackers with cheese. Let everyone serve themselves. This is a cocktail party, and I want the guests to mingle and talk."

Wanda nodded and did as she was told. She began to fold the scarlet napkins, noticing the coordinated color theme of red and white throughout the apartment.

"I love the floral arrangements and all the red and white you have going on."

"You can appreciate that, can't you, Delta queen?" Romeo responded.

"I like it, but you didn't do it for Delta."

"No, but my boyfriend is a Kappa, and it's our anniversary, so I wanted to honor our time together with his colors. I hope he'll appreciate the sentiment."

"You are too much. I'm sure he will appreciate it."

Every detail was essential to Romeo. Everything had meaning and purpose. He would have been a successful interior or stage designer. Romeo dreamed in technicolor and, when presented with options, could visualize aesthetic coordination. The apartment was a theater of color and gaiety, including fine linen, candles, and fragrant red geranium floral arrangements.

"Should I give the party favors out when they arrive or leave?" Romeo asked.

"Don't you normally do it at the end? What are they?"

"I have personalized wine glasses for everyone who RSVP'd, a wine stopper, and an elegant keychain bottle opener. Let me show you the cute boxes I wrapped them in."

Wanda stopped folding the napkins and followed Romeo into the bedroom to see the party favors. "Oh, these gifts are so precious," she said. "What are these twisted little baggies on top?"

"Those are special edibles I got from my friend in Colorado. That's why I want to give them out right when guests arrive."

"What do you mean?"

"They're edibles. THC-infused chocolate kisses."

"Yeah, you need to give those out before the party, but you better let everyone know."

"Look, this is a small, intimate party, I know everyone who's coming. Getting high was a requisite on the invitation. I originally wanted to have a marijuana-tasting party with all kinds of plants for people to imbibe."

"Romeo, I think that would be a bit much. At least wait until it's legalized before you do something like that. Either way, you must tell them when you hand them out; you don't want someone eating that chocolate and not knowing. Besides, you don't want them fighting over the hors d'oeuvres when they get a serious case of the munchies." Wanda and Romeo laughed at the thought.

"You're right, I wouldn't do that. I'll hand out the

edibles…baggies and give the boxes when they leave."

"You need to give me mine now," Wanda said.

"Go ahead. Here's yours."

"Actually, I'd better wait till later, I don't want to get all paranoid and anxious around people I don't know. Is your friend—the one you wanted to introduce me to—coming?"

"He'll be here, but I didn't mention anything to him, so you can decide what you want to do after I introduce y'all."

"That's fine. Blind dates can get messy, you know."

"It's up to you. You'll like him. We'll see."

* * *

About an hour later, most of the guests had arrived. Romeo had emphasized in the evite that it was an intimate cocktail party between six and nine. Wanda was having a conversation with a chic lesbian couple, one of whom was pregnant. The other was a curvaceous diva flashing the most magnificent manicure with talon-like nails painted in iridescent colors that sparkled like the crescendo to Fourth of July fireworks. They were telling Wanda about their experience with artificial insemination and why they decided to do that rather than adopting.

Wanda talked about her interest in adopting and the challenges she would face. "I've spent time in South Africa and just love it there. I'd move there in a heartbeat; there are so many expatriates. While I was there, I investigated the adoption procedures, and it turns out to be much less expensive and cumbersome than here."

"I would love to go there; it's on my list. I hear it is beautiful. Cape Town, they say, is like southern California," Tatiana, one of the women, said.

"Exactly," Wanda responded. "Will and Jada, Oprah, a lot of celebrities have homes there."

The conversation detoured into a discussion about natural birthing clinics that sounded more like spas than delivery rooms. The couple attended prenatal yoga classes and were praising its benefits for exercise, relaxation, and improved sleep.

Romeo, the consummate host, was circulating and introducing guest who weren't acquainted. "Wanda, let me introduce you to my friends," Romeo said, approaching from behind with a tall distinguished mixed gray-haired man with a matching beard and another strikingly gorgeous young man with dark skin and short-cropped platinum blond hair. As they got closer, Wanda noticed the darker skinned man's green catlike contact lenses. Automatically, she did a double take, turning from the lesbian couple to directly face the three men. Romeo, the Marvel superhero look-alike, and the other, more distinguished guy. Romeo introduced them to her as Reynaldo Evers and Tyrone Davis. "Reynaldo is the best dentist in town and the richest, I must say, if you want your grill done, he's the man. Didn't you do Lil Wayne's teeth?"

"He's one of my patients," Reynaldo replied.

"And this is the one I told you about, Wanda. The rest of you know Tyrone. Isn't he gorgeous?" Romeo said, with his arm around his boyfriend's waist.

"Nice to meet you. I've heard so much about you," Wanda responded, turning to Tyrone but diverting her eyes from his paralyzing glare, like high beams from an approaching car. She extended her hand.

"My pleasure," Tyrone said as he turned toward Tatiana and Jade, kissing each on their cheeks.

Wanda turned to face Reynaldo and said, "I don't know about a grill, but I can always use a good dentist."

"So nice to meet you," Reynaldo said.

Romeo continued with the introductions. "Tatiana, you and Jade have met Reynaldo, right?"

"Yes, of course we've met. How've you been, Reynaldo?" Jade asked as she leaned in for a kiss on the cheek.

"Yes, that's right, we met last time I was here. I see things have changed since then. Congratulations, when is the baby due?" Reynaldo asked, looking directly at Jade's midsection.

"November. We've got a few months."

"Good luck. Make sure you get a lot of rest—you'll need it. Sleep deprivation is the cost of love, for a while."

"Oh, don't I know it," Tatiana said, shaking her head.

"You all enjoy and try some of the appetizers. They're delicious and the signature drink, the green cosmos, will blow your mind," Romeo said.

"OK, we will," everyone said.

"Everything is just lovely," Jade added.

"We're going to circulate; I want to introduce Tyrone to Max Haperstein and his wife. You know they have their modeling agency, and they're always looking for talent. Come on, Tyrone, let me pimp you out," Romeo teasingly said.

"Shut up, Romeo. I just met Wanda. You're embarrassing me." Tyrone laughed.

"Wanda already knows you're a slut," Romeo said as he nudged his boyfriend's shoulder playfully.

"She doesn't know nothing but your lies. Don't pay attention to him, Wanda."

Wanda smiled as the two of them left to engage with the other guests, gently and playfully slapping each other on the arm with limp wrists.

After some small talk, Tatiana said, "Well, good meeting you, Wanda, and seeing you again, Reynaldo. We're going to get something to munch on and try those drinks Romeo was raving about."

"Speak for yourself. Mine will be a virgin," Jade said. "That's the one thing I miss, and I don't dare eat those chocolates Romeo gave out."

Everyone laughed. "You'll have plenty of time after November for that. You'll probably appreciate it more then," Reynaldo said as the women walked away.

"So, Wanda, are you here alone?" Reynaldo asked. Before she could answer, he continued by saying, "How do you know Romeo?"

"Yes, I'm here by myself, and we've been friends for years. We actually grew up together. I'm slightly older than him. In fact, I used to babysit him back in the day. We also went to the same college."

"You went to Columbia?'

"Yes, for undergrad and grad school."

"Impressive. Business, Law?"

"Neither. Communications, media relations— journalism."

"Nice. Everyone I meet these days is in either law or banking—MBA types doing the Wall Street thing."

"Not me. I decided to go a different route. Presently doin' some independent work with social media companies and individuals. Mostly content for podcasts, blogs, and other postings."

"Good for you. How come we haven't met before?"

"I don't know. I haven't been here that often. Last time was about a year ago for Romeo's Halloween party."

"I didn't make that. I heard it was a blast."

"So, you're a dentist. How do you like it?"

"It's a skill that I've gotten better at and built a practice over the years. It's been fairly successful," Reynaldo said.

"Who are the celebrity clients Romeo was talking about? Lil Wayne?"

"Yes, somehow the word got out that I did grills in Brooklyn, and the word on the street can be the best marketing possible."

"Any female entertainers come to you?"

"I get a few. Most are wannabe rappers—the Love and Hip-Hop reality-show types. Most trying to make a name for themselves, so they go to the extreme. Get paid and self-indulge on a hundred-k mouthpiece. I don't judge. They want to spend their money; I'm not their financial planner, but it is amazing. Most of the women give their money to the plastic surgeons for manufactured rear ends and headlights, not grills, if the car analogy holds. I figure I should get my share so when they come to me, I am more than willing to oblige."

"That is so interesting. Love and Hip Hop and the Housewives shows are my guilty pleasures."

"I used to indulge when it was reality, but it's all scripted now and the same repeat storyline, so I stopped watching. It's rather trite and predictable."

It wasn't love at first sight, but there was a mutual attraction, and the haze from the marijuana kisses lowered their inhibitions. As the evening progressed, they spent more time with each other than with the other guests. The possibility for more was set that evening. Near the end, Reynaldo asked Wanda for her number. As he was creating Wanda's contact, the phone rang and she noticed a woman's name, Maria, appear on the screen.

"Excuse me," Reynaldo said to Wanda, and he stepped away to take the call. When he briefly returned, he apologized for the interruption but gave no details about the call.

Wanda gave him her number, and he entered it into his

iPhone. "I'll text you, and you can add me to your contacts. I really enjoyed your company this evening, and hopefully, we can get together soon."

Wanda took his statement to be sincere. Out of the corner of her eye, she noticed Romeo looking and smiling, sensing that he had successfully made a connection that evening. "I look forward to that. Please stay in touch. Who knows? I may want my grill done one day."

"I hope not. It has been an absolute pleasure, and I am so glad I met you this evening. Unfortunately, I have an early appointment tomorrow, or I would stay longer and continue our talk." He leaned in to kiss Wanda on the cheek. Before turning toward the door, he approached the host, Romeo, to say goodbye. "Hey man, thanks for inviting me, but I have to head out. Early day tomorrow. Everything was great. Actually, things went better than I imagined."

Romeo looked quizzical and furrowed his brow before saying, "And how is that?"

Reynaldo responded with a slight nod and tilt of his head toward his left where Wanda was standing. She had her back to them and clearly was unable to see Reynaldo's motion. Romeo confirmed the sentiment by saying in a low voice, "We'll talk."

* * *

By 9:30 p.m. everyone was gone, leaving just Wanda and Romeo to clean up. Tyrone left with the Hapersteins to go to another party in the building, telling Romeo he would be back shortly.

"OK, where should I start?" Wanda said.

"Just pick up the glasses and plates and put them in the kitchen sink," Romeo said.

"Everything turned out great. Seemed like your friends thought highly of your get-together—no pun intended."

"Yes, they didn't want to go. Luckily, I had enough food. Once those munchies hit, there was a line at the buffet table. I almost had to tell them to leave," he said jokingly. "You know, I had to cut Max Haperstein's wife, Margaret, off those cosmos. She had about four in less than an hour, not that I was counting, but she can get messy. The Jewish couple. you met them, right?"

"We briefly spoke. They own the modeling and talent

agency, right?"

"Yeah, that's them. She's an alcoholic, and I didn't want her to humiliate herself or me if she acted out. She's a nasty drunk and likes to take her clothes off when she's had one too many. Max's a little freakish himself. He likes to watch—a voyeur. Word is he encourages her to bring young men home and all kinds of shit, swingers and who knows what else. They are rich as hell—just rich white people with kinky afflictions and privileges us regular folk can't imagine."

"Get out. They act so sophisticated. And her outfit—it was Christian Dior couture. If she took it off, I would have grabbed it and run out the door.

"Girl, I know, but I would have been right behind you fighting for it," Romeo added with a hearty laugh.

Wanda finished collecting the glasses and plates and sat down next to Romeo on one of the stools by the kitchen center aisle, "Everyone was dressed so nice. It was the most diverse party I've ever seen. Gay, straight, black, white, able, disabled. It was so nice. And how sweet was Little Ralphie when he sang Adele's song 'Hello.'"

"Ralphie can sing his ass off, and he gets around in that

wheelchair better than some people who walk. He ate two of those chocolate kisses, so I know he was feeling nice."

"Yeah, those edibles sneak up on you, but it was a mild high. Just right for this type of gathering . . . just a light buzz. I saw him whipping around. I was afraid he might hit somebody. How do you know him?" Wanda asked.

"I got the mellow ones. It's amazing the different types of plants, different grades of THC, and how they make you feel. We definitely should get a license to distribute when this stuff goes legal.

"Ralphie, he lives on this floor. We just met going in and out on the elevator. He's got the best drugs in the building; everybody knows him. I don't ask questions, but I know he was incarcerated, and I think he suffered the injury—spinal cord—while in prison. Rumor is he got paid millions from the city for his injuries."

"That's so sad. I feel so bad for him. I can't imagine not being able to walk," said Wanda.

Romeo continued, "Don't underestimate him, he's mad strong. You see his upper body with that tight shirt he was wearing? Built like the Rock…those arms!

"I was hanging out with him one night; we went to this neighborhood bar, and these white fraternity-looking boys were drinking and taking shots. At first, everything seemed friendly enough, but things changed, and they started getting too familiar and teasing Ralphie about how they were going to tip his chair over. We overheard a slur about me and him, something about who was the bottom, me or Ralphie. He had had enough and was a little tipsy when one of them started rubbing his head. Ralphie lifted himself out of the wheelchair with his arms—you know, his legs are paralyzed and atrophied. He flew in the air about three feet, grabbed on to the boy who had rubbed his head. The boy tried to run away, with Ralphie on his back and legs dragging across the hardwood floor as he held on. The boy had this terrified look on his face.

"You thirsty want something to drink?" Romeo abruptly says to Wanda in the middle of telling the story.

"Yes, are you high, finish the story!" Wanda says.

"OK," Romeo says as he goes to the refrigerator to retrieve beer for himself while asking Wanda what she wants.

"Just ice water is fine," Wanda responds.

"And yes, I'm a little toasted," he says as he grabs the beer and Wanda's water before returning to the stool. "Where was I? Oh yes," he says asking and answering his own question before Wanda could respond. "They both fell to the floor with a crashing thud. Everyone in the whole place got up and started to encircle the two. Ralphie put the guy in a chokehold like a UFC match, and the boy almost passed out. People started yelling 'He can't breathe! Let him go!' and trying to pull Ralphie's arms apart, but thank God, he finally let go. I just looked with my mouth wide open; I couldn't believe my eyes, and there was nothin' I could do.

"The boy's friends were going crazy; it was chaos. Some of the people helped pick Ralphie up and put him back into his wheelchair. The guy's friends lifted him up and helped him to the barstool. He was conscious but slumped over with his head on the bar. One of his buddies was trying to get him to drink some water, lifting his head because he couldn't do it himself and feeding it to him, but it was spilling down the front of his shirt.

"Ralphie was laughing. His demonic laugh was creeping everyone out as they stood there in shock, staring at him, trying to process what had just happened. Ralphie finally broke the tension and, Ralphie being Ralphie, yelled 'Drinks on me!'"

"Oh my God, it must have been insane. No cops?" Wanda said.

"No cops, thank goodness. We left a while later, but before we walked—rolled—out, he did a wheelie with his chair, spinning, making a screeching noise from the rubber tires on the wooden floor. He was laughing like a fool in the middle of the bar. It was my worst nightmare and the best night ever for him. Now when he goes there, he is so respected; they save a table for him in the corner, and if someone is sitting there, the bartender or waitress will ask them to move, saying it is reserved for the handicapped, like a parking space.

"I think he was in some gang back when . . . Bloods, Crips, or some group affiliated with them. But he's good to me, so I don't question his past. I don't go out with him anymore, though. It was the craziest night I ever experienced."

"That's some story. Damn, that Ralphie is a character," Wanda smiled, having imagined what it must have looked like as Romeo was telling the story.

"I know. I really can't do it justice; you had to be there. It was so ironic—this disabled paraplegic taking down this young, strong, able-bodied man. I am sure that dude will think twice next time before he makes fun of someone with a disability. Anyway, enough 'bout Ralphie. What about you? I saw you and Mr. Reynaldo getting it on. How did it go?"

"He's good. We talked. He's charming, interesting; we have similar humor, talking about the different folks at the party. What's the real story? I felt hints of mystery, which is sexy but sketchy."

"What do you mean? He's out there, single, attractive, rich. I told you he was married, been separated . . . I think he's divorced 'bout five years now."

"Where's his wife—ex? Is she still in the picture? Do they still see each other?"

"I know they had a nasty divorce. She wanted his money. Lucky, he had a prenup. They eventually settled all their issues. No kids, so that didn't complicate matters. I think she moved to California."

"That's good to know. He is easy on the eyes and is in fabulous shape. Nice bod, clear skin, and obviously nice teeth; being a dentist and all, I guess they're his. He looked much younger than his age. You said late fifties; he looked more like someone in their forties."

"I hear that, sister. Plus, age ain't nothing but a number! He reminds me of that guy in the Dos Equis beer commercial—the most interesting man in the world. Mixed gray hair, tall, thin, deep-set penetrating hazel eyes."

"That's funny. So, what do you know about ex-wifey? What was she like?"

"She was fun, good humor, the more effervescent in the relationship. Reynaldo can be quiet and serious at times. She was always in high spirits. Puerto Rican, attractive, good hair—you know the type. Basically, light-skinned straight-haired black girl . . . Latina. Her name was Maria. I forget her maiden name—probably Rodriquez, Ortiz, something like that. You know, them Spanish names."

"Oh, Maria? When we were exchanging numbers, his phone rang, and I saw on the screen it was from Maria. My reaction was 'Here we go, another player with a stable.' I assumed it was one of his honeys and hesitated about giving him my number."

"Are you crazy? I hope you did. You don't think a fifty-year-old man isn't going to have a past?"

"I did. You know me—I do not have time or energy to be competing with these girls out here. So, I guess that's who was calling. That's different, unless it's another Maria. You don't know her last name; it could be anything. How am I gonna do my online stalking if you don't know her name?"

"Girl, stop. You have to ask Reynaldo about all that. I'm sure y'all will be talkin' 'bout everything," Romeo said with a smirk. "You know, he gave you a thumbs up before he left. He winked at me and nodded his head at you. That told me everything."

"Speaking of the devil, he just texted me," Wanda said.

"See, I told you. What'd he say?"

Wanda read the text aloud: "Wanted to thank you for the conversation and company this evening. Put me in your contacts, and let's stay in touch."

"Uh-oh, girl, he's on the hunt. You go, girl."

"Please, he's just friending me. I'm sure he's got hundreds."

"We'll see. You have got to stop being so negative; it's not like you. Things will work out if you let them. The universe bends toward happiness and fulfillment if you let it," Romeo said.

"Yeah, I guess you are right. Thanks for all you do and your genuine concern. For you, I'll try and be more positive."

Wanda stayed a little longer, doing dishes and straightening up. She replayed, in her head, the exchanges she had with Reynaldo and relived the excitement and pleasantry, in her heart, she experienced that evening. She left Brooklyn Heights in a mellow, gracious mood. A lovely social gathering and an attractive man. Dreamlike images and future thoughts had already begun to percolate.

Chapter 8

It was a lazy, quiet Saturday afternoon, and Jordan was home alone in front of the TV with his mind in another space, when his younger son, Jared, unexpectedly stopped by. Jared was distraught and needed to get things off his chest, so he eased into a discussion, but not until he had staked his position by suggesting how misunderstood he was. The victimization posture transferred cause of his state of mind to something other than himself. It also allowed for therapeutic probes without directly implicating the victim. The door opened, and both crossed the threshold together initially.

"I do understand your anger and frustration. I felt the same at times, but for different reasons," Jordan said, in response to Jared's claim of misunderstanding.

"Do you really? How can you know what it's like to be

me? I am different; people think I'm weird—a nerd. I never seem to fit in. Always by myself. I have no genuine friendships. Chad used to be a fuck-up, you sent him to military school for two years, and he always lands on his feet. I try and do everything right—school, career, marriage, live up to and by everyone's expectations. But everything is screwed up. Chad has a halo; I have horns. Why me?"

Jared had always been more dependent on his parents (needy) than Chad. One of the upsides of military school was that it instilled independence and self-reliance in Chad. Jared, on the other hand, always sought his parents' approval. As rebellious and independent as Chad was, Jared was just the opposite. The idea that two children from the same parents could have such distinctive personalities made Jordan contemplate the possible reasons. In the competition for gene superiority, Jordan would take credit for good qualities and assign the bad to Trina. Likewise, Trina did the same. However, it was not unfathomable, if you considered that Jordan and Trina were different in so many ways, that the kids would have distinctive personalities.

The differences became more apparent as the boys got

older. Jared was more book smart and inclined to prefer math and science to politics and social sciences, as was Chad's inclination. Their career choices reflected their different aptitudes. Measured by general career "success" standards, Jared had done better than his brother. He completed college in four years; Chad dropped out after two. He was an analyst with a private equity firm and had a bright future. Chad's future was still undefined as he catapulted from one thing to the next. In spite of such accomplishments, as well as being the father of two beautiful children, Jared constantly questioned his self-worth. He was afflicted with low self-esteem. Growing up, he admired and loved Chad beyond reproach. The three-year age difference meant that phases of development overlapped. Jared was a rational, logical thinker; Chad was more creative and intuitive. Jared was on the chess team. Chad was a varsity athlete in track and football when he returned to public school after military school. Jared made the honor roll every semester and was accepted to the University of Penn's Wharton School. Chad attended the state university.

In spite of everything, Jared was always known as Chad's little brother—a shadow he never escaped. There were other things that affected Jared's personality. He was a good-looking kid, but not as physically attractive as his brother. He was always overweight, and he even went to a fat camp in Arizona for support and counsel one summer to address his eating disorder. No psychologist could identify what caused an individual's personality disorder. It was not necessarily one thing as much the cumulative effect of many. Trying to identify the causal effect of any one of a multitude of things was scientifically impossible. Life was about winning and losing, chaos and order; one hoped that, in the existential randomness, the wins outweighed the losses. One had to be a skeptic when someone claimed his or her life was so perfect. Even so, in the end, no matter who you were, we were all going to die—such a fate none could avoid.

If that weren't enough, his wife, Juanita, was the cause of Jared's recent despair. She manipulated his good nature and took advantage of his love and admiration for her. Her spendthrift ways and selfishness left Jared wanting.

"Look, son, you can't compare yourself to your brother because you are unique and separate individuals—plus he wishes he had the things you have. He has said so many times how much he admires you. We have never compared you two or loved one more than the other. We love, accept, and respect you both because of your individuality. You should own that. You have such talent, Jared. I know firsthand that life isn't easy. I believe that we all, at some point, ask life's big questions and reflect when we compare ourselves to others. Believe me, my life has had its own serious challenges."

"Challenges? What challenges? You seem to always have it together. What are you talking about, Dad?" Jared questioned with concern. He and Chad were too young to have been made aware of their father's past, but given the circumstances and the situation at hand, this was the perfect time: a teachable moment. As parents, they had always been protective of their boys, insulating them from their marital ordeals.

Jared continued. "I mean, just look at your houses, your career. You're a lawyer and now a professor. I have always felt the pressure to measure up because of you and Chad, and I don't feel like I do and never did. I never felt like I was enough, no matter what I did. I always depended on you and Mom for approval and support. It wore me down after a while, and when you question your self-worth, you lose your confidence."

"Maybe we shielded you and your brother too much, but

what if we hadn't supported you the way we did? Would you have preferred that? I'll tell you one thing; I grew up without that level of support and was forced to be independent, which at times made me feel alone and unloved. I didn't want you and your brother to experience that. You are my son, and believe it or not, we are the same. It took me a while to find my bearings, and there was a lot I had to overcome before I liked—loved—myself. You will find it; trust me. I have confidence in you."

Father and son had crossed a threshold that they'd dare to tread in the past. "I do need help, and I know that you and Mom have done well by us, and believe me, I appreciate it, but my issues are not just about love. It's the difference that I feel, the constant gloom and depression that leads to other problems. I lack that brightness and clarity that others have, and it hurts. I have constant doubts and questions that are easily triggered by others' opinions. I feel that I am a single step away from it all crashing down," Jared said.

"Maybe we need to think about professional help, son. The way you're talking reminds me of what your mom went through, and lately, I've noticed a resurfacing of things I thought she had overcome . . . like depression, a constant sadness. Part of it is age, and I think the other is her personality, which will likely always be there. When we were younger, she exhibited the feelings you're describing, and for years she seemed to manage the sadness and its darkness, but it lingers and always will. We must learn to manage our disorders, son; no one is perfect. We all have our demons. There is no real normal, son," Jordan said, continuing to connect with and console his son.

"That's what disturbs me the most, Dad—the stuff I can't seem to control, and the consequences it causes."

"Son, you're not giving yourself enough credit for your own self-awareness. That is most telling about you. The fact that you are aware of your flaws and their consequences is one thing, but your desire and ability to overcome them is another. You should take pride in that, son. Now I feel you're ready to hear my story—to learn about my life's challenges. It's a good thing you're sitting down."

"Thanks, Pop. All right, what do you mean?" Jared said with a smile as he sat up in his chair looking attentively and waiting for Jordan to continue.

Jordan hesitated for a moment to choose how to begin. He

swallowed heavily and said, "Son, do you remember the time that you boys stayed at your grandmother's for a while? You were about five years old."

"Yes, I remember."

"Well, your mother and I were going through a difficult time then. We separated because your mother found out that I was having an affair."

"What?" Jared exclaimed.

"Yes, son, it's true. I was a stubborn, self-centered narcissist and hurt her—a deep pain that she will never forget. I became callous and disrespected not only your mom, but you boys, our family. I stained her faith, love, and the purity of the life we had built together. To this day, I don't understand how she stayed with me. She could have easily walked away, and she did for some time . . . that's when you three were staying with your grandmother. I am eternally grateful to her for standing by me and allowing me to do right by her, earn her trust again.

"You see, I went through my own dark period where I did things—things I'm not proud of—that led me to having that affair. Eventually, I sought professional help, well after everything fell apart. I wish I had done so sooner. I was able to talk about the things that I knew I couldn't handle on my own anymore. In retrospect, everything bottomed out before I started to put it back together. We are all fallible, son."

Jared was mesmerized and somewhat embarrassed for his dad, and himself, that he was hearing this. It had never occurred to Jared that his dad had done something like this. In his eyes, his dad was the epitome of virtue and strength. It was unimaginable that a separate truth existed. He had experienced a similar dissonance when his parents told him that Santa was a fantasy. *How could this be?* Jared thought.

"Son, there's more," Jordan continued. "I was drug addicted."

"No . . . Dad . . . What are you talkin' 'bout?" Jared gasped and held his dropped jaw.

"Yes, son, I was addicted to crack cocaine and had reached the lowest point in my life. I lost my job. My career was in shambles; I was in a deep depression. I even contemplated suicide. Thankfully, I was able to retreat from the edge because I realized that there were so many important, unfinished things in life. You, your brother, my grandkids, and your mom are my anchor. Your mother is my salvation. Lucky for me, I came to that realization before it was too late. You, on the other hand, are a self-aware, intelligent guy who can get help before it gets to that point. I was staring into darkness with no options. You have options, son."

"Wow, I had no idea all this was happening, and I still can't believe what you're saying. It sounds surreal."

"Oh, trust me, it was real. It's not something I'm proud of. I haven't spoken to Chad about this and would not have told you, but for the fact that you needed to hear it and are old enough to understand in the context of everything. Life is fraught with good and evil, and there are no guarantees, son. We all have another side. When you get to be my age, you will be thankful for the simple blessings and the fact that you are a survivor."

There was silence for some time, and neither initiated a word. The poignancy of the moment was best appreciated in solitude. Jordan reached out his hand to Jared, and Jared clasped it tightly. They both got up from their chairs, and the father held his son securely, whispering in his ear, "I love you.

"Keep this between us, son. I shared this with you to let

you know I have faith in your strength and character, and no matter what, you are and will continue to become a better man than me. And that is a blessing. No father can ask more from his son."

"I got you, Pop, and I'm going to look into finding a therapist."

"That's my boy. Let me know if I can help. Now, tell me, how are my grandkids and Juanita?" Jordan asked.

"Kids are fine, growing up too fast. Aisha is doin' good in school and active with soccer and gymnastics. Little Sean is getting bigger every day and getting into everything—you know those terrible twos."

"Ah, that's great to hear, son. I am so lucky to have such great grandkids. And Juanita? How is she? I feel like I haven't seen her in a while."

"Juanita . . . she's OK," Jared replied hesitantly while scratching his head. He continued, "Umm, Dad? When you and Mom had your problems, how did you handle them? How did you stay together?"

"What's going on, son?"

"Well, Juanita hasn't been well; that's why she hasn't

really been around."

"What do you mean?"

"I don't know; it's hard to explain. She complains of headaches and says she can't sleep. Her doctor prescribed a sleep aid, but now she takes it daily. It has side effects and is starting to get out of hand. She's always moody and irritable. Sometimes, she sleeps in the spare bedroom or on the downstairs couch because she says she needs her space."

"That's not good."

"Yeah, I know. I just don't know what to do. We fight a lot. She says she wants a divorce, Dad. I don't want to do that, especially because of the kids."

"How do you handle that? Have you sought counseling?"

"Yes, we're seeing this woman, Mary something; she's a family counselor. Juanita always mentions divorce whenever we argue. What did you and Mom do? How did you make it through all that you just told me?"

"There is no one way or right way, son, but we had you and Chad, and your mother and I are different in many ways, but we are the same when it comes to family, our values, and our commitments. I can't say for sure that we stayed together just because of you boys, but we both realized that our lives and overall well-being were better together than apart. How's your *relationship* with Juanita?"

"Relationship? You mean sex? We don't . . . she's sleeping in the spare bedroom."

"That's not good. It's no wonder you're depressed. Now that I think of it, she seems distant around the family. I've never seen her embrace your mother like a typical daughter-in-law would. Your mother has encouraged Juanita to call her Mom, but she doesn't. If they were closer, perhaps your mom could try to talk to her, approach her about this. I'm useless; this is something another woman would be better suited for."

"Dad, I'm not asking you to do anything. Plus there's nothing you can do; we have to work this out ourselves. I'm willing to do the work, but it feels like she's got one foot out the door. One day she loves me, and the next she's sleeping in the other bedroom, saying she needs some space."

"What does she say exactly?"

"She mostly complains about my job because I practically work seven days a week. She says she feels like she does everything—raises the kids *and* works and rarely sees me. I get that, but on the other hand she has no problem running up forty thousand in credit card debt."

"Whoa! That's a lot."

"Yeah, and we fight about it, and she gets mad, and when she gets angry, she just charges more stuff. I guess it's the way she copes with everything. It's a vicious cycle."

"You've got to get hold of the situation, son. Is the counseling helping at all?"

"It's early. We've been meeting separately and talkin' after our sessions. Some days things seem fine; other times, I really can't tell."

"I hear you. But stick with the counseling, and maybe you guys need some time away together. The last few years haven't been easy—getting married and having babies right away. Your mom and I can watch the kids. Talk to Juanita about it and let us know. And keep me posted on how things are going. I'm here for you if you need to talk."

Jordan was feeling emotionally exhausted, but the floodgates had opened, and one other issue was worthy of bringing up. "On another matter, your brother called your mother the other day, and she said that it seemed like he's having money problems, and he hinted that he wanted to come home. I don't think it's a good idea for him to stay here because we don't want to enable him. He's almost thirty; it's time to grow up. We'll see—he hasn't spoken to me about anything yet," Jordan said.

"He hasn't said anything to me about that, but I'll call him and see what's up. Anyway, I've got to run, Dad. I have a conference call to prepare for that's in an hour. By the way, last night, I told Aisha that I was seeing you today, and she wanted to come. She gave me this picture she drew and told me to 'give this to Papa.' He handed his dad a picture from a manila folder he was carrying. It was a drawing of a little brown-skinned girl in a red dress holding a yellow flower under a magnificent round, orange sun. At the bottom it said, "I Love You Papa, Aisha."

Aisha's self-portrait and love note warmed Jordan's heart, but Jared's struggle was also transferred. He had no answers to the situation.

Chapter 9

Chad, Jordan's older son, was living in the Maryland/DC area after dropping out of college and sojourning from job to job for the last eight years. He had taken some certificate courses and was working as a writer, trying to make a living freelancing. He had also spent the better part of the last five years maintaining a journal and writing a novel. He was encouraged to pursue writing by his aunt Wanda, who had noticed an aptitude at an early age. Between the two boys, Chad, the older, had proven to be the most difficult to his parents.

* * *

As a young teenager about seventeen years ago, Chad was resting in the back seat of the family's Mercedes and feeling pensive. Jordan was driving, and Trina sat quietly in the passenger seat. Jordan was preoccupied with a stream of unconscious thoughts, and when the silence was broken by a comment or observation from Trina, his only response

was "Ahem. Umm. Uh-huh" at appropriate intervals.
In spite of his programmed responses on cue, she
challenged his listening skills, just to let him know she was
on to him. "You haven't heard a thing I said, have you?"
Chad was accustomed to the banter and paid little attention
to his parents quibbling; after all these years, the fact they
were talking, regardless of the substance or lack thereof,
was a good sign. He was preoccupied with his own
personal situation and ambivalent about going to a military
boarding school in New England—leaving his family and
particularly his mother, Trina. Chad was a complex child in
spite of the security, love, and attention his parents gave
him.

The challenges appeared early, starting in elementary
school. Jordan recalled on numerous occasions telling the
story, lightheartedly, of how Chad was sent to the
principal's office on the first day of kindergarten. Jordan
received a call from Trina to meet her at the school because
Chad had urinated on another boy while in the boys'
bathroom. It was later determined that the boys had a piss
fight, and each was soaked when they finally settled the
duel, having run out of ammunition. It was basically a tie.
When Jordan arrived, the principal said, *'This is a first'*
because she had never experienced a situation like this, in

which a kindergartener was sent to her office for discipline on the first day. Later, Jordan would jokingly tell Trina that he realized then that they should have set up a bail fund for Chad and a college fund for Jared.

Chad was not a bad kid, but impulsive—he lacked impulse control and rational prudence and was a risk taker. Consequently, he frequently found himself in some dilemma whose outcome seemed to go against his interest. After Chad was expelled from his second middle school in two years, Jordan and Trina were advised that regimented discipline (military school) was best for their son. Remorseful, and without resort, Chad accepted his fate. He was anxious about what the experience at a New England military school would be. He was also uncertain about his parent's motives. *Are they giving up and sending me away to avoid the embarrassment I cause them?* he thought.

The school sounded like a prison to him, and it just didn't make sense in his mind. It didn't help that neither his father nor mother could give him a satisfactory explanation. Chad, being strong willed, was already contemplating an escape plan—to run away from the academy to somewhere no one would find him. It would be his revenge for their decision to abandon him.

The academy was based on a boot camp military philosophy of discipline and regimented order. Cadets had considerable hours of individual psychoanalysis with the core team of psychologists/educators. It attracted a very rich and notable clientele, sons of professionals, businessmen, and entertainers, many of whom had behavioral problems brought on by the disease of privilege and wealth—spoiled kids' syndrome. Some of the cadets were diagnosed with ADHD and prescribed psychotropic drugs like Ritalin and Prozac to control their attention disorders and hyperkinetic behavior. However, this was not Chad's diagnosis.

Upon their arrival, the campus's expansive, tree-lined grounds struck Trina. Its gothic buildings were nestled magnificently against the rolling Berkshire mountain range. Cadets were assigned to help new recruits move in and assisted with the luggage. Trina took care of the registration and other administrative details before they all went to Chad's room. When they entered the room, Trina remarked on the airy spaciousness. The room had oversize arched windows with distinctive partially beveled glass panes at the upper reaches. It faced the western sun, whose unblemished rays were shining into the room. The rays were refracted from monochromatic to rainbow tinges of color as they penetrated the prisms of the beveled glass. There were two beds in the room each set off to one side, two desks, and a reading area with a bookcase; outside the room was a large multipurpose common area and adjoining shower room to accommodate all the cadets on the floor. An American flag prominently hung in the common area.

After helping Chad get settled—hanging clothes in the closet and folding others in drawers—it was time for Jordan and Trina to leave. Chad had a roll call shortly. His roommate had not yet arrived. Trina tried to comfort Chad and detected his fright and discomfort. He dreaded the moment his parents would leave.

"You will meet new friends, honey. This will be a wonderful experience that will prepare you to go to the best schools in the country. It's lovely here; everything is going to be fine. I promise," Trina said in an attempt to console her son.

Nothing Trina said penetrated Chad's fear or sadness while he strained not to cry—a brave thirteen-year-old facing a new experience with no previous reference point. He was unanchored and unmoored and asked to be self-reliant where no self-reliance existed. Jordan, who was standing off to the side, motioned to Trina to go. He felt emptiness in his stomach at seeing his little boy straining to be strong under the pressure. He moved to hug him and whispered to Chad that they would be back to see him in a few weeks, and there was no need to be afraid.

Trina and Jordan kissed Chad goodbye and left to drive back to New Jersey. He watched from his window as the car pulled off and drove down the long roadway out of the gated grounds. He pulled down the blinds to his window and lay across the bed. Chad was downcast, alone, and feeling deserted. He would spend the next two years at the military school, but he looked forward to the summers at home.

* * *

Chad grew to be a handsome young man; military school was in his past and had been supplanted by many other experiences. He had obvious and prominent influences from his father; most people remarked how much he looked like Jordan, in both facial and body structure. Chad wore his naturally curly hair in twists and had olive skin with high cheekbones and a shadow black beard. His dark features, deep-set eyes, baritone voice, and swagger were distinctive and confident and together projected an air of intrigue.

In college, before he dropped out after his sophomore year, he was very active in political affairs and community organizations. He was a member of an organization that was post Black Panthers and pre-Black Lives Matter. Barack Obama's election had a major impact on Chad's political philosophy. He became a voracious reader of radical political dogma. He read Frantz Fanon's *The Wretched of the Earth*, Albert Camus's *The Rebel*, and *The Autobiography of Malcolm X* and studied the Black Panther movement and Huey Newton's life in the sixties and early seventies, Tupac was his favorite rapper.

Chad was, at that time, living in the Maryland/DC area with a lovely, supportive strawberry-blonde Irish girlfriend. She had porcelain white skin with natural pinkish lips that matched the pink nipples and areolas on her breasts. Chad met her at a black student rally on campus; she was as obvious as a white pearl surrounded by a necklace of black ones. He later discovered that she was not just an activist attending a rally but an officer, the secretary of the Progressive Students Society—previously known as the Black Students Union. An earlier lawsuit against the exclusivity of race-based and other types of associations had meant that whites could join otherwise segregated

student associations. And Megan proved to be politically
astute and cool enough to become a member and officer.
She was the Rachel Dolezal of her college, without the
guilt of cultural appropriation. Her progressive political
philosophy and feminist views coupled with attractive good
looks proved to be of undeniable appeal. Different from her
wealthy father, and maybe because of him, a staunch
Republican who sought to maintain the purity of their Irish
ancestry, Megan's mantra was "Let's Make America
Brown." She loved and believed in her lover's idealism and
causes, so she was willing to have her daddy unknowingly
finance her romantic idealism.

Chad asked himself years later if he had loved Megan
and was unable to answer the question. There was no doubt
that he had cared for her and was romantically entwined.
But at the time of their romance, they were at different
levels of personal development and had different goals.
Megan came from privilege and wealth and, as a result,
could aspire to and visualize greater heights than Chad. He
was of a black middle-class upbringing but nowhere near
the generational wealth of Megan's family. He was
consumed with personal needs like food, shelter, security,
and constant uncertainty. Megan never dealt with those
incidentals. Her life as a well-traveled trust-fund baby had

skipped the lower rungs of need. Megan's aspirations were naturally directed toward more lofty pursuits. She could dream bigger dreams without concern of failure if they did not materialize—essentially riskless. Her energies and imagination were limitless. Her pursuit was self-esteem, worthiness, and self-actualization—that which wealth and class privilege afford people of her ilk. It is something few minorities can grasp. Ironically, as she was a progressive feminist with an immense worldview, Chad, by association, was able to broaden his perspective on the world and political events.

It was some eight years since President Obama's 2009 inauguration, and Chad was reminiscing about the hope and change of the election, as opposed to the doom and gloom of the present with a new president. The period of the Obama presidency, coupled with his aligned and ever-growing political awareness, seemed so distant now. He remembered how excited he had been that bitterly cold day in 2009. The air of optimism and community spirit was palpable as he walked with the endless crowds to the Capitol's great lawn ceremony. He still had the Obama T-shirt and other memorabilia he bought from the African American street vendors lined along the parade route. The words and emotions he read and felt from the struggles of

African Americans in the past all seemed to converge at that moment. The history he had immersed himself in was being played out in real time, and he was a part of the grandeur of a new beginning. Chad recalled the Million Man March, which he and his father had attended, and the awakening he felt back then, as a child, part of a crowd of like-minded people, protesting for freedom and racial justice. Being of and part of something bigger than oneself.

Obama represented so much to so many, and Chad would be touched by the moment like so many others for the rest of his life. The resurrection of Martin, Harriet Tubman, Malcolm, Frederick Douglass, and the multitude of slaves, civil rights leaders, and hopes and dreams of the masses were embodied in Obama's oath of office. Once he was sworn in, there was a thunderous rejoicing and silent tears of joy as everyone exhaled the greatness felt and witnessed. It was a busy day; a lot happened that memorable day to all of us and, in particular, to Chad.

* * *

The hope and optimism of Chad's early twenties had faded over the years. The intellectual and financial support of his girlfriend had ended long ago as she graduated and moved on to more macro global initiatives and started a movement dedicated to confronting climate change and poverty worldwide. The Bill and Melinda Gates Foundation funded her new initiative. As Megan moved on, Chad struggled in the wading pool trying to make ends meet. He even had a stint as an Uber driver in an attempt to earn more money to pay for rent and food. He maintained contact with his mother and Jared and, indirectly, with his father through his mother. Fierce independence and growing introversion kept him away. A tattoo in Chinese characters on his left anterior pectoral muscle symbolized his determination and rebellion; it could be interpreted as "Never Surrender Your Ideals to the Will of Others."

Eventually, Chad transitioned a passion for writing into a source of income. To be a good writer, one had to be an avid reader. Chad had mastered both talents beginning at the military academy, where he found refuge in books. As a result, he was working independently as a magazine journalist, writing news articles and features for a variety of publications.

Writers live a solitary life, which suited Chad, especially because he was an introvert. His introversion was not stereotypical shyness or social awkwardness. He was outgoing, affable, and highly attuned to other people's moods, both good and bad—he intuitively felt everything, sometimes too much. Emotions that others managed as a daily dose of life, such as anger and anxiety, exhausted him. He was more at ease with less tension and more love. People like Chad had been labeled empaths or intuitive and tend to be creative because of their nonconformist nature.

A lot of his solitary time was spent writing his novel about coming of age as a young African American male. He had sent out query letters to agents about the book but hadn't gotten any positive responses. The rejections accumulated in a third-floor attic room he was renting from an elderly couple. He kept them all and used them to motivate his efforts. Eventually, at a point of extreme frustration and lack of money, he called his brother, Jared. They had remained in touch over the years even though extended periods of no communication did occur. But Chad would, without fail, call on his niece's and nephew's birthdays and holidays to send his well-wishes. His brother lived a comparatively stable lifestyle as a banker with a major firm. Soon after Jared had met with their father that emotion-filled day, Chad called.

"Hey bro, how you been?" Jared asked. "We miss you. Mom and Dad are really worried about you. Are you all right?"

"Yeah, I'm OK. just figuring things out. I talked to Mom, but you know Dad and I have our issues," Chad responded.

"Yup, both of you are the same—independent . . . solitary."

"I don't know about that, but how are you and the family? My niece and nephew—they must be getting big."

"We good. Yeah, they're growing like weeds. When are you coming to see them?"

"I was actually thinking about moving back to the area. You know I've been trying to make ends meet down here. It ain't easy. I'm Ubering, got some freelancing assignments, finishing up my book and sending out queries, but when you're a new author, publishers aren't willing to invest in you unless you can show that you have a huge following on social media. I got a hundred followers on the 'Gram, if that. Maybe if I change my name to Steve Harvey, I'll get my book published."

"Yeah, too bad we don't have Harvey or Kardashian money, huh? Speaking of which, how are your finances?

Mom said you were struggling."

"Not good, bro."

Jared had anticipated Chad's call from the conversation with his father and had spoken to his mother about the same. He assured Trina that if Chad needed a place to stay to get back on his feet, he would offer. He also assured his mother that he would be able to manage a short-term stay and would actually enjoy having his brother around.

"I'm sorry to hear that. You are welcome to stay with us for a while…until you get on your feet. I have a spare bedroom in the basement. It's private, so you'll have your own entrance. This way you can continue writing and not worry about paying rent; just give me what you can. And, honestly, it would be great to have my big bro around, and the kids can get to know their uncle better. I can help out as much as I can. How much time do you think you need?"

"Man, that sounds great. Are you sure? I miss the family and appreciate the offer more than you know. I'm not sure how long . . ." Chad's voice trailed off.

"You know what? Don't worry about it. We will take it one day at a time. We miss you, man. I'll tell Mom and Dad the good news."

Chad got his affairs in order in DC and moved in with his brother some three weeks later. As planned, he was able to continue working on his book and freelance on the side. He was grateful to be able to reconnect and mend the discordant family strains of the past decade.

Chapter 10

It had been several months since Wanda first told her family about her intention to adopt, and now the time had finally arrived. She was at Liberty International Airport waiting to board a flight for Cape Town, South Africa, with Dr. Reynaldo Evers by her side. Yes, they had developed a relationship since meeting at Romeo's party. Wanda was comfortable enough to call him her boyfriend. Their courtship flourished to relationship rather quickly—they were as loving and trusting as couples who had been together much longer.

From the beginning, probably because of their age and maturity, they weren't interested in and didn't have any patience for adolescent games, so they were sincere and forthright with each other and set aside insecurities and vulnerabilities for truth. They discussed politics, culture, and lifestyle. The conversations, late-night phone calls, and time spent with friends were mutually shared and appreciated.

Wanda recalled an early dating occasion when they went to dinner at an expensive restaurant in Manhattan and were discussing politics. She asked Rey, "So where do you get your news?"

With a straight face, he responded, "FOX. What about you?"

Wanda told her friends that she felt faint and couldn't eat her food. Fortunately, before she could scream, he laughed and followed with, "I'm just joking. You should see your face right now. I follow CNN mostly, but I like my girls on MSNBC—Rachel Maddow and Joy Reid."

Wanda was so relieved that he was joking; it had not crossed her mind until that moment that politics could really be a relationship killer. The idea of spending time with a right-wing Republican was nauseating. This was not the only hiccup they confronted during their courtship. Naturally, past lovers and his marriage/divorce were topics of discussion. One evening while at his apartment, they ordered Chinese and were binge-watching episodes of *House of Cards* when a scene came on in which issues arose in Frank and Claire Underwood's marriage, forcing

Wanda to grab the remote and pause the show to ask, "So what exactly happened to end your marriage?"

"Whoa, where's this coming from? What do you mean?" Rey responded.

"I want to know about her. What was she like? I mean, who was she? How did you meet . . . what happened? I think I deserve to know," she said inquisitively.

"You really want to know the details? Fine, I'll tell you. We met at a party in Harlem. It was her birthday; my friends were throwing a party—not for her birthday, but they made it part of the party. I hadn't been in a serious relationship for some time, and we just hit it off that evening. She was in a relationship that wasn't working out, so we started dating after the party. The stars just aligned, I guess."

"Did you love her?"

"Well, yeah, obviously, babe. I mean, what kind of man would I be, marrying a woman I didn't love? We spent eighteen years together, three years living together and then fifteen married. We separated and tried to reconcile for about two years. After we separated, we would still hook up because we enjoyed each other's company. The sex was good, but we realized that the love had vanished. We didn't know it then and tended to fool ourselves somewhat, hoping to recapture what we had, but we knew that it would never be the same. It was inevitable that we would divorce."

"But what went wrong? Why didn't you have children in those eighteen years? I know how much you like kids."

"Well, that was another issue. We tried, but she couldn't get pregnant. We did infertility treatments, had sex when she was ovulating, and we even tried insemination, but we learned that she couldn't have kids. Once we had exhausted everything and it was apparent that it wasn't going to happen, it affected her deeply, more her than me. I was willing to adopt, but she didn't want to. The whole thing made her feel inadequate. There was always the need to comfort her, and she needed extreme love and constant reassurance. It became too overwhelming. I later learned that her childhood was tragic and scarred her for life."

"What do you mean? What happened to her?"

"I don't really want to get into the details because it's her personal life and not mine to share with anyone, but I'll just say that she was abused by her father. He was an alcoholic and used to take advantage of her."

"My God, I can't imagine how she dealt with that throughout her life."

"Yeah, I guess she never really healed. That and the fact that she couldn't conceive just added to her self-esteem issues. She always felt she was damaged, unworthy."

"Wow, that is so sad."

Rey got off the couch and went to the bedroom to retrieve a photo of his ex-wife that he kept in a shoebox with other old memories. When he returned, he handed the photo to Wanda.

"This is my ex-wife."

"She is gorgeous. You two would have had some cute kids."

Rey chuckled. "Thanks. Her name is Maria Velez."

Wanda froze. She realized that Rey's ex-wife was her brother's former mistress. Years ago, Wanda had uncovered, through a friend, that her brother was having an extramarital affair with a woman named Maria Velez. The affair had rocked Jordan's marriage and almost destroyed it and him when she shared her knowledge with Trina. For years, Jordan had blamed Wanda for what transpired, and only in the last few years had they reunited and mended their estrangement.

"I know your wife. She was in advertising, right?" Wanda said.

"Wait, how do you know her?"

"She dated my brother while he was married. She broke up his home, and I got dragged into the entire mess."

"What? When we first met, she told me about her relationship with a married man. That was your brother?"

"Yes, unless she was seeing some other married man. His name is Jordan Baros."

"I don't recall his name, but it could have been. Wow. This is crazy."

"I knew this was too good to be true. Now what am I to do?" Wanda stood up and started pacing back and forth.

"Hey, now, what's with all the theatrics? Come here; sit back down."

Wanda returned to her seat next to Rey, looked him

straight in the face, and said, "Your ex-wife was my brother's mistress. Was she the one that called you at Romeo's party when we were exchanging numbers? I saw the name Maria appear on your screen."

"Babe, that was years ago. And yes, that was her. We are friends. It doesn't matter and has nothing to do with us now. I'm sure your brother is over it; I can't imagine someone holding on to something like that this long. What's he gonna do—shoot me because I married his mistress?"

"It's just so awkward and unexpected. Who knows? He might try and kill you; he was in a bad way when she left him. You know how those soldiers have PTSD," she said sarcastically. She laughed at what she had just said while Rey just frowned.

"So, what happened to her? Where is she now?" Wanda continued.

"Well, there was a series of events that made things worse. Her mother passed after years of illness. She never really recovered from that, and she left town after the divorce. We stay in touch; I used to help her out financially. That's what she was calling about when you saw the name, promising to send some money I had lent her a while back. It's a small amount, no biggie.

Saying nothing at the moment, Wanda uncrossed her legs and sat on the couch with her head in her hands supported by her elbows resting on her thighs like two pillars while looking directly at Reynaldo.

"She lives in California, the San Francisco area. She was working in the beauty and fitness industry where she was on TV doing hair infomercials on the Spanish channels, YouTube, and some magazines ads. The product she sold damaged customers' hair drastically, and there was a class-action lawsuit, but the company filed for bankruptcy. Not only that, but Maria's hair fell out."

"She lost her hair, so sad," Wanda said.

"She was receiving treatments for her scalp, trying to restore her hair. It was bad. We lost contact for a while. She was probably emotionally distraught and embarrassed. When I tried to call her, her number was disconnected, and she never replied to my emails. She even took down all her social media accounts. Basically disappeared . . . abandoned everyone until recently. Seems to be back on her feet. I don't get into details. I think she's living with someone—another woman. As I said, I don't ask too many questions; we have both moved on. It's better that way."

* * *

The flight attendant announced, "Flight number two-seven-three-five to Cape Town, South Africa, is now ready for boarding. First-class and United priority customers are welcome to board."

"That's us," Rey said. They grabbed their passports and unlocked their cell phones to pull up their digital boarding passes to be scanned at the podium.

"Here we go, babe," he added as he attentively assisted Wanda with her small Louis Vuitton carry-on bag the other luggage having been checked in earlier.

At one point during the long flight, Wanda looked at Rey while he was asleep and felt happiness softly envelop her without fear. She had never felt so loved, secure, and needed. She embraced the moment and felt the totality. The complementary emotions engendered by Rey and expectations of her new baby overwhelmed her. The thoughts brought a smile to her face and an internal rejoicing in her soul—a choir of hallelujah joy.

They were staying at a five-star hotel in Cape Town. A limousine was waiting for them after they landed, got their luggage, and went through customs. Both were exhausted after the sixteen-hour flight. It was a twenty-five-minute ride to the hotel; they held hands and admired the sights along the way. Wanda thoughtfully reminisced about experiences and feelings from previous trips to South Africa. Rey looked out the window, taking in the new sights and cataloging the sensations in his mind.

"It is still as beautiful as ever, but the water shortage is so acute they may start to ration usage. When I went on the state department website, they cautioned about rising crime rates. This is clearly one of the wonders of the world. I hope it remains so," Wanda said.

"In a simplistic way, I understand why the Europeans, although driven by greed, fought so hard for the beauty and wealth of this land. Nothing justifies the inhumanity and apartheid for gold and minerals, but human history is replete with colonization and exploitation of others for land, natural resources . . . wealth."

"Listen to you, Doctor. You sure your doctorate wasn't in political history?" Wanda teased her boo. "Two minutes in South Africa and you're ready to relive the revolution."

She chuckled. Rey nudged her and smiled.

"We have to visit the museums, and we definitely have to go to Robben Island where Mandela was imprisoned. I can't wait for you to see the richness and beauty of this country contrasted with the most horrific ugliness humanly possible," Wanda said.

Rey nodded approvingly, appreciating the beauty and charm of her intelligence.

They arrived at the hotel and were met at the entrance by a bellhop who greeted them and graciously loaded their luggage onto a cart. He directed them to the front desk to register. The bellhop waited to escort them to their room. As soon as he opened the door, they were struck by the beaming sunlight from the southern coast of the Indian Ocean and the airiness of the room. Rey did a rand (the South African currency)-to-dollars calculation in his head and handed the bellhop what he thought was an appropriate tip. The bellhop continued to hold his palm out for more. Rey gave him another hundred rand, and the bellhop smiled, nodded, and turned to exit the room.

"How much did you give him?" Wanda asked.

"I don't even know," he laughed.

"What's the exchange rate? How many rand for a dollar?" he asked Wanda since she was the expert on everything South Africa.

"I think it's ten rand for one dollar," she replied.

"Ms. South Africa should know, not think she knows," he joked.

"You zip it," she lovingly snapped back.

"Well, we have five bags, and I gave him hundred rand. But at first, I gave him ten, and he didn't like that, kept his hand out. I'll get it together soon enough. I probably gave him too much," Rey mumbled as Wanda laughed out loud.

"The baby's delivery isn't until Thursday next week. I have to meet with the social worker and adoption agency on Wednesday. They want us to stay and spend time with me and the baby for a few days before we leave on the twenty-third. So, I figured that we can vacation and tour the country until then. How does that sound?"

"Perfect. Exactly what we hoped to do," Rey replied.

"I want to take you to the east coast area to the penguins' reserve. They are so cute, and we should go to this restaurant called Oceanside; it's to die for because of the setting, and the food is amazing. Afterwards, we can walk on the beach until we get to the point where the Indian and Atlantic Oceans meet. We can straddle two different bodies of water. Even the temperature changes!"

"It all sounds good. Look at you, the romantic planner. When do you want to go to Robben Island?"

"Ha ha, yeah, I'm trying to romance your pants off," she joked and continued. "I want to do some shopping for the baby tomorrow. You can maybe go to the seaport walk to explore, eat, people watch . . . unless you want to come with me?

"No, I'll hang out with the people at the seaport have a drink and people watch."

"OK. I figured that we would do Robben Island next week, and if you're up to it, we can go to the wine country and take the lift to Table Mountain, which is one of the main attractions in Cape Town. And as for our last day before baby Africa comes, we can go to the animal reserve on the Cape of Good Hope and run from the baboons."

"Sounds great. I like it, but are you serious about running from baboons?"

"Yeah, babe, and they can be vicious. People feed them, so they get comfortable showing their asses and pink little penises to people."

"Showing what?" He laughed.

"They are a mess; they even jump on your car. They are wild animals, you know. We'll get to see other game— ostriches, monkeys, and even giraffe. You'll enjoy it."

"Sounds like fun except for the baboons."

"Don't worry, I'll protect you." Wanda giggled.

* * *

For the next five days, they had a ball doing everything they planned—exactly to the plan. Everything was working out beautifully, and they couldn't have been happier. Soon they would welcome the baby into their lives, but they had a few more things to experience. Cape Town had several well-known natural resources. One of the most popular was Table Mountain, which was part of the Table Mountain National Park.

"Do you want to hike up or take the cable car lift thing?" Wanda kiddingly asked Rey.

Rey bent his head back so far he almost fell backward looking to the top of the mountain that touched the clouds in the sky, "You're kidding, right?"

She laughed and grabbed his hand to stand in line to take the cable car to the mountain's peak. Once at the top, the breathtaking view of the entire city was quite the sight. As they walked the trails at the top, they stopped to take pictures and selfies and saved them to post on social media because they didn't have cell reception on the mountain top. In the gift shop, they purchased some picturesque postcards as memorabilia for friends, family, and themselves. It was memorable and something they would treasure long after they left South Africa.

After leaving Table Mountain National Park, they headed to Boulders Beach and walked along the warmer Indian Ocean part of the beach, contiguous to the much cooler Atlantic waters. They strolled silently barefoot, sandals in hand, feeling the white granular sand softly prickling the bottom of their feet, like an acupuncturist's needle pinch healing a tender muscle. All five senses were active and vibrant. They took deep breaths in and out and enjoyed the intoxicating smell, sound, and sight of the turquoise blue ocean with dolphins leaping in the distance.

They allowed the moment to be imprinted forever in their memory—the instant spoke louder than any words they might say about their mutual experience. Eventually their walk along the beach led them to the African penguins' reserve.

"They are so cute with their little natural tuxedos," Wanda said.

"They really are, and there's so many of them! This must be penguin heaven, where they get to sun on the beach and lay on these granite rocks. They are a different breed than those in the South Pole."

"Honey, this is so great. You see why I could live here?"

"Yes, it's beautiful. But all this magnificence is killing me—climbing mountains, walking beaches . . . we need to eat and drink. Aren't you hungry?"

"Oh yes, I can definitely eat. You should've said something earlier, baby. Let's go to the restaurant I told you about; it's actually along the beach. It has the freshest seafood. It's Asian cuisine—sushi and other stuff."

"Sounds good. How far?"

"Not far. We can walk it. We'll take the path outside the

reserve; it leads straight to the restaurant."

"Hope I can make it. Let's go," Rey said humorously.

The restaurant's décor was of plush African print furniture. It had an uninterrupted view of the luminous Atlantic Ocean with sounds of the waves crashing against the shore. A tall blonde Scandinavian-looking hostess with menus in her hand led them to an open veranda with a table in the corner close to the shoreline. It was near dusk, so the bright orange sun was descending against a crescendo of colors on a fading blue canvas of African sky. Everything on the menu was straight from the ocean.

"Do you like oysters?" Wanda asked.

"I like the way they taste, but it's the texture that I have a problem with."

"I know. A lot of people say that. You don't feel the same 'bout sushi?"

"No, for some reason I don't. I guess fresh sushi doesn't feel as slimy as oysters."

"Well, I'm going to order the oysters. You want to share a platter of sushi and sashimi?"

"Yeah, that sounds good; we can share. Let's order a bottle of their best pinot noir. The South African wineries are actually some of the world's finest."

"OK, you know your wines, and I know how to drink, so you order, and I'll drink," Wanda said.

"You better share the wine with me." Rey chuckled.

A young black waiter, dressed in black pants and a white shirt with a black vest, came to the table and introduced himself. "Hello, welcome to Boulders Bay and Oceanside Restaurant. My name is Okafemu, and I'll be your waiter this evening. Can I get you something to drink to start—off our wine list, perhaps?" he said, with a distinctive British accent.

"We'll have water with lemon and a bottle of your pinot noir, Paul Cluver."

"Excellent choice. I'll get that started while you study the menu. Any appetizers before I go?"

"Yes, I'll have the oysters, please, a half dozen," Wanda added.

"Very good. Anything for you, sir?" Okafemu asked Rey.

"No just the wine. That's it for now, thanks."

"OK, please relax and enjoy the lovely sunset. I'll be back with your drinks and appetizer."

"Did you notice the diversity in this country? It's truly amazing, I think I've seen every nationality and race in the world. When you think of Africa, you picture images of bare-breasted black Africans. But the reality is that from the north to the south, Africa is the most diverse continent on the planet. We grew up with such false narratives. The infrastructure, education, and sophistication are so much more developed than we were led to believe. I was looking around at breakfast in the hotel, and I overheard so many business deals and discussions. There were a lot of Asians, so I assume the Chinese are in South Africa big time," Wanda pointed out.

"Not just South Africa. China is flexing its muscles everywhere. With one-point-three billion people, they are a force to be reckoned with. America better step its game up," Rey said.

"Yeah, these people are not playing." Wanda paused and then said, "Isn't it gorgeous this evening? I told you."

"Today was spectacular, and everything has been great

so far. I'm really excited for this meal. What are we doing tomorrow? Cape of Good Hope and hanging out with your baboons?"

"Tomorrow the cape and then Robben Island, and on Wednesday, we will rest up before we get our little baby, and life is changed forever," said Wanda.

"Changed for the better . . . a new chapter. Are you ready to be a mommy?"

"That sounds strange and wonderful. I guess. How does one know? I know it's what I want. I'm really excited about being in the delivery room. They said they would give the baby to me after delivery. The mother says she doesn't want to hold the baby at all, which has me a little upset because I can't imagine carrying a baby for nine months and not wanting to see or hold it when it comes into the world. It seems so unnatural."

"I don't think it's normal, but maybe she is afraid if she holds the baby, it will be harder to give her up. Who knows?" Rey said, speculating on something that had no answer.

Okafemu returned to the table with Wanda's oysters and the wine. He presented the bottle to them, uncorked it at the table, and poured a sample for each of them. They moved their crystal glasses gently to swirl the wine, smelled the fruity aroma, took a sip, and nodded to the waiter to continue with the pour. He then placed a basket of sweet potato bread with olive oil on the table, compliments of the house.

After they ordered the deluxe entree to be shared, Okafemu said, as he retreated from the table, "Enjoy. Your meal will be out shortly."

Wanda savored the oysters doused with lemon and topped with horseradish and a *Tabasco* sauce while Rey dipped his bread in the olive oil. After a while, Okafemu returned to clear the table and place a decorative platter of seafood in front of them. The assortment consisted of tuna tartare atop sushi rice; prawn tempura with cucumber, avocado, and fish eggs; and a luxurious amount of lobster tempura, asparagus, crabmeat, and avocado, surrounded by an assortment of lavender-and-white orchids as garnish.

"This is so beautiful that I don't want to mess it up," Wanda said to the waiter as refilled their wine glasses.

"Speak for yourself," Rey said as he picked up a piece of seafood with his fingers and leaned back to ingest it before Okafemu finished pouring the wine.

Wanda shook her head at Rey as she began to service both their plates, and politely inquired of Okafemu which tribe he was a part of.

"I am Zulu," he proudly proclaimed. "We are the largest ethnic group in South Africa. The history of South Africa, its culture, and tradition are highly influenced by the Zulu people. The Zulu warriors under Shaka carried out major victories against the British colonists. Our spears and courage defeated the guns of the Brits."

"I am aware of the bravery of your people before apartheid. You must be proud," Wanda complimented.

"Thank you, and yes, I am. You are Americans, right?"

"Yes, how can you tell?"

"The way you talk, plus I watch a lot of TV. Bill Cosby, *American Idol, The Wire.*"

Wanda and Rey smiled. "Yes, but the United States is not exactly like the TV shows," Rey said.

"I know. I intend to visit New York one day; everyone says it's the greatest city in the world. I've traveled throughout Europe and attended school in London but have not been to America yet."

"That's where we're from—the New York area. When you do visit, please let us know," Rey said and handed Okafemu his business card.

"So kind of you, thank you. I will definitely let you know when I visit. Please enjoy your food, and I'll check on you later," Okafemu said, backpedaling and bowing as he left the table.

"That was nice of you," Wanda said to Rey.

"I'm building my international coalition. Maybe expand my dental practice to South Africa."

"Hopefully not your grill implants," Wanda joked.

Rey, who had been eating during the conversation with Okafemu, laughed and said, "This is the freshest, bestest seafood I've ever eaten. They must have just caught it."

Wanda took a bite. "Oh my God, this really is very good. It's orgasmic," she responded.

The couple enjoyed their evening together embraced by the warmth of fading golden rays of the setting sun in concert with nature's orchestra of sound from the monkeys and birds that occupied the National Reserve. After dinner, they stood by the veranda posts looking out to the water and starry night sky and sipped the last of their bottle of wine. The magic of Africa was omnipresent as they stood there. Rey's arm securely hugged Wanda as her head pressed against his shoulder. Wanda felt as if she were in a Jonathan Green painting with its vivacious colors showcasing a woman in her yellow petticoat dress holding a colorful red parasol as she pranced on the banks of a streaming southern river headed to a larger outlet, as it had done since creation and would continue into eternity. The painting was titled *Doin' the Charleston*.

* * *

Wanda and Rey for the next two days continued their itinerary as planned. They visited the Cape of Good Hope and saw the ostriches, buffalo, and zebra that freely roamed the land. The baboons were actually respectful, except for one who tried to sexualize one of the females. He mounted her back with no shame and seemed to be twerking, but she was not having it and turned, screeching a high-pitched sound as she moved away, slapping him in the process.

"You go, girl. Hashtag MeToo," Wanda yelled,

laughing at the same time. Everyone in the tour group laughed with her.

"That's funny. Female baboons objecting to sexual assault. Animals got rights too. Look, he's showing his penis to her." Rey laughed. "Now I know there's a link between man and apes; they all like to show their junk."

In spite of the fun of it all, one moment resonated more than the others. No matter how many times Wanda had visited Robben Island, she always walked away emotionally drained. The spirits of experience were even more profound for Rey, given this was his first time. It was a harsh island outpost, and before it was a prison, it was a leper colony. It sat six miles off the coast of Cape Town in shark-infested waters. Wanda and Rey traveled by ferry filled with other tourists to the historically infamous site. Mandela, affectionately known as Madiba by South Africans—a term used to describe a wise and elder tribal chief—was sentenced to prison for sabotage in 1964. The inmates of Robben Island were political prisoners: Nelson Mandela, Walter Sisulu, Pan African Congress founder Robert Sobukwe, and other patriots who had fought against apartheid. Plaques with biographical sketches were outside each of their prison cells.

The cells were depressingly tiny cramped spaces with small cots. Mandela's cell had a desk. The bleakness, hardship, and suffering of the men imprisoned still haunted. It was unimaginable how the men survived such harsh conditions. The prison represented a testament to the fight for human rights, based on years of merciless suffering endured by men of principle led by Mandela. And in 1997, with Mandela then the president of South Africa, the island became a museum and a historical site. The guides were all former prisoners, sharing their personal agony while giving the tour.

Chapter 11

The day had come. Wanda was to receive her baby. She had a restless sleep because of competing emotions— excitement, love, and fear, as well as bliss and anxiety. She tried to mediate the conflict, but it was useless.

"How are you feeling?" Rey asked, "You didn't sleep at all last night."

"I'm tired. No, I didn't. I couldn't. I have too much on my mind. We have to be at the hospital at nine-thirty. We'd better get ready."

"It'll be fine. Don't stress. Try to think positive and feel excited. I can't wait to see our baby girl."

The phrase 'our baby girl' resonated with Wanda, and it meant more than its literal interpretation. It seemed that Rey had become as invested in the adoption as Wanda. It was a moment of emotional transference that added to the elasticity of their relationship.

She would witness the birth this morning, so thoughts regarding the birth and the birth mother's feelings took residence in her mind. Wanda wondered what the precious moment of birth would be like for the birth mother, after caring and nourishing the baby to term. The mother's experience was in contrast to Wanda's relationship these last few months, centered on sonograms she received periodically from the agency. Today, the sonogram images would become a human being, and she would get to hold her baby girl and take her back to America. She pictured the first moments being full of joy, but self-doubts regarding her ability to nurture and protect the baby also entered her mind

"I don't know what feelings I have; there are so many! I feel like shutting down and curling up into a ball."

"Relax, honey, this is going to be one of the greatest days of the rest of your life. Take it in steps; it will naturally come to you. It is a good thing. Enjoy your moment." His voice and wisdom were consoling. Wanda wondered if she could have forged ahead with her decision without the strength and support that her relationship with Rey had given her these past few months.

They arrived at the Cape Town hospital and were directed to the maternity delivery ward. Rey retreated to the waiting room, and Wanda was prepped and escorted to the delivery room. The birth mother entered into the sanitized white delivery room shortly thereafter, and in short order, Wanda witnessed the miracle of birth. The details and process were a blur, but the one thing she remembered was the seemingly loud cry of life, the cutting of the umbilical cord, and a nurse handing the baby to another to bathe and remove the placenta.

"It's a healthy baby girl. Seven pounds, three ounces," the nurse said, looking at Wanda.

The joy of it all was like no other she'd ever felt. The nurse handed the soft-cotton-towel-wrapped baby to Wanda to hold in her arms for the first time. Tears of happiness and joy streamed down her face. The beauty of it all, whether she realized it or not, would be everlasting. However, the ethereal moment abruptly ended when the nurse took the baby, a few minutes later, from Wanda to place her in the pediatric viewing room.

"We will need you to finish some paperwork. You can go and let your husband know the good news. What is this beautiful bundle's name?"

Surprised by the reference to "husband," Wanda replied, "Imani."

"Very good, such an exotic name," the nurse said and, with professional dexterity, took the baby to continue her care.

Wanda removed her hospital clothing and went to meet Rey in the waiting room. He greeted her with an embrace as she entered the room.

"She is gorgeous," Wanda said, tears of joy still settled in her blushed eyes.

"I know. The doctor told me. I'll get to see her in the nursery. How are you feeling? How was it?"

"Honey, it's all a blur. People were moving around—it went so fast. I remember hearing her cry, and the next thing I knew, she was in my arms, and I broke down into tears. I am still in good shock."

Rey finally got to see the baby in the nursery, and like a proud dad, he beamed with pride. They finished the necessary birth records and left the hospital to prepare for when they would bring Imani home.

Wanda sat in the car, silently contemplating something the social worker had said. It was mentioned in the paperwork that the mother had a seventy-two-hour right under the law to change her mind. She didn't share this worry with Rey. They returned to the hospital every day to see the baby. They held her, fed her, and changed her diapers, sharing thoughts on her alertness, weight gain and adjustments she was making so quickly.

Chapter 12

It had been three days since Imani's birth. The mother did not reassert her parental rights, so Wanda's concerns were tempered, and Wanda and Rey spent their first night in the hotel with the baby. The sense of purpose, warmth, and love overcame the strange uniqueness and sleepless nights. Rey slept as normal, but Wanda, normally a heavy sleeper, reacted to every coo and whimper of baby Imani. And on schedule, as instructed by the nurses, she maintained the hospitals routine and fed her newborn baby formula at 3:00 a.m. Just as the stars align and shine their brilliance on us, clouds invariably interrupt the illumination with their overcast. So it was when Wanda was holding Imani on the balcony of their hotel room looking at the forest greenery on Lion Head Mountain off in the distance. It was a call from Jordan, whom she had not spoken to since leaving the States.

"Hey, Jordan, how are you?" she asked.

"Better question is, how are you? I assume you're a mommy now?"

"Yes, I'm a mommy, and you're an uncle. Her name is Imani Baros. I apologize for not calling; it's just been a bit overwhelming the last few days. I'm so glad you called. I actually intended to do so today."

"I completely understand, and please don't apologize. I'm just glad that everything worked out. I can't wait to see my niece."

"We're scheduled to leave on Monday, so we'll be home soon. It's been wonderful, but I can't wait to get back home and into my bed. The hotel is nice, but it's not a place to raise a child, particularly a newborn. We have to see the pediatrician today, and after that we are free to go."

"We are looking forward to meeting the baby, but you tell us when. We don't want to overwhelm you—we can wait until you settle in." Jordan momentarily hesitated, then said, "Wanda, don't get alarmed, but there's another reason I'm calling." Wanda noticed a distinct change in Jordan's tone of voice, and it set off an instinctive reaction in her as she waited for him to continue. "Mom was admitted to the hospital again last night."

"Oh no! Oh my God, what happened? Is she OK?"

"Luckily, she called me earlier and said she wasn't feeling well, so I went over and took her to the emergency room. The preliminary diagnosis is that it's another stroke. They are running some tests as we speak."

"This is the second one in the last two months. Jordan, I'm so scared," Wanda said.

"The doctor also asked if she had fallen recently because there are bruises on her right arm and hip."

"I don't know if she's fallen, but she's unstable and bumps into things often. I don't think she can feel much on her right side. What are we going to do?"

"Nothing we can do for now; she's under the care of the doctors. I'm going back this afternoon to visit. I am so sorry to have to call and worry you with this, but I didn't want anything serious to happen and you not know what was going on."

"Please don't even go there."

"I know. Well, anyway, Trina wants to say hi, so I'll pass the phone to her, and I'll see you next week. I'll call you again if I get any new information. I'll tell Mom you'll be home soon with the baby; that'll get her spirits up. Here's Trina," Jordan said as he handed the phone to his wife.

"Hi, Wanda. I've been listening to everything. How are you, girl?"

"I am exhausted from the delivery room, caring for Imani, and just the idea of being a mommy. I can't imagine or even pretend to know what giving birth is like."

"It's a beautiful experience, but definitely more exhausting and difficult than anything I've ever done in my life. Totally worth it and absolutely rewarding. I am so happy for you. How's Reynaldo doing with it all?" Trina said.

"He's cool as ever; nothing phases him. He takes in all in stride. He's been my rock. I can't wait to see you, and Imani says hi."

"Aww! Tell my niece her auntie Trina loves her and can't wait to see her. Don't worry about Mom. They think it's a mild stroke, a TIA, but they are concerned about her blood pressure and trying to get it down. Thankfully, they caught it in time. I think once you get here it will cheer her up, but I feel like the doctors have it under control for now."

"I know it's a tough time. I know you guys are doing your best. Thank you for all that you're doing."

"Don't worry. We'll let you go back to taking care of Imani. I know you have your hands full, and we'll see you when you get back next week."

"OK, yeah, she's right here sleeping in my arms."

"You make sure you get your rest. Remember, you have to adjust to the baby's schedule because they do not respect yours. Also, tell Reynaldo I said hi and congratulations. Oh, one more thing. Jordan and I are just curious—how is the baby flying next week? I know it's a long flight."

"Yes, that was an issue, but we've arranged special accommodations. She'll be in an incubator-type contraption for the flight. Everything will be fine. And thanks. I will try and rest. We'll see you soon," she said.

After hanging up, Wanda just sat with her baby snuggled against her breast, holding her even tighter. No tears, just thoughts of life and death. They were not abstract thoughts, but the reality of both—her new baby in her arms and her mother lying in a hospital bed.

Chapter 13

Sonya had applied for the position as Jordan's research assistant, and just as he had promised, she got the job. They began working together and quickly found a rhythm that allowed for good productivity on the projects. Jordan, as the director of the university's Black Male Project, was inspired by President Obama's initiative "My Brother's Keeper." He recalled attending the White House when President Obama unveiled the program and described its purpose as an idea that had occurred to him in the aftermath of the killing of Trayvon Martin. Trayvon's death sparked a national debate about race and class. He recalled the challenge the president had made to the country to ensure success for young men of color as a "moral issue for our country."

Jordan applied for and received a grant to pursue programmatic changes within the university in order to remedy particular maladies that affected young men in post-secondary education. The theme of his presentation to the African American Educational Society was specific intervention that would increase retention and enhance graduation rates of African American males from colleges. One of the main objectives was identification of at-risk students and early intervention. There was statistical data from particular schools of successful best practices.

"We are making good progress, and you've really done great work in pulling articles and researching abstracts in academic journals. The only thing left is to button this up by making sure that the citations and format are in order. You know how detailed and specific the MLA requirements are. Also, the paper has to be converted into a PowerPoint for my oral presentation."

"I know. I can work extra hours if you need me to. The research is complete and supports your theme. I have a few more articles that I want to read through, and don't forget you said you need more statistics on low-income underrepresentation in college—disproportionately black and Hispanic."

"Yeah, I need to be clear about the urgency of the matter and the failures to address the issue. Then we need to make specific recommendations. We'll get there."

"For the recommendations, I'll look into what other campuses have done and their successes."

"That's a good look. Let me know what you find."

"I don't know if you want to use it, but I found this paper by Dr. John Wimbush, a psychologist and the director of the Johnson Black Cultural Center at Brown. He questions why some refer to black males as endangered animals subject to extinction and then uses that analogy to frame the issue and remedy. I have it right here. I'll read it to you," Sonya said as she shuffled through her papers. "'One, the number of the species must be limited; two, the predator must be identified, and three, a remedy must be offered to protect the species.' He goes on to say, 'I think it is interesting that this country uses terms reserved for animals to refer to black males.'"

"I like that. It exposes the racism that is at the crux of a lot of this. Let me see the article."

Sonya handed him the article, feeling proud of herself, and said, "You know what? I have to tell you . . . I'm really grateful for this opportunity. I really enjoy working with you, and I've learned so much."

"Education can be fun when there's a passion and

purpose to the work. Make sure that in the future, if you have to write a term paper or do research, it's something that interests you. The quality of your work will be better, and the intellectual journey is so much more satisfying. The fun is in the process. I guess the same applies to work and careers. If you are doing something you love or enjoy, it doesn't seem like work. Plus, you get paid."

"Word. I hear that. I'll sit down with you later this week and talk about the recommendations. My son is sick, not sleeping, so I've been dealing with that."

"Nothing serious, I hope?"

"No, it's not serious. He's in day care, and the kids pass stuff around, and then he brings it home, and everybody gets it. He'll be all right. I kept him home today. My mother is taking care of him."

"If you have to take care of your son, you should go home. That's a priority; you know you get family leave from me," Jordan said with a smile.

"Oh, thanks, professor, it's fine. Plus, I can work from home if needed."

"OK, you decide. We're getting close to the end. How

are your other classes?" he asked as he thought about how their particular project would extend into the summer.

"I'm doing well in my classes, maintaining a three-point-eight GPA. I just have to get ready for finals, and I have a group project I need to finish up."

Jordan was hesitant in hiring Sonya, knowing how attracted he was to her. He rationalized the decision on other considerations particularly work demands and Sonya's intellectual abilities. But his rational had limits, the foremost being reality. "When this is over, I think we both deserve a drink," Jordan proposed.

"Yes, indeed I would love that," Sonya replied without hesitation.

Sonya's eagerness sent an adrenaline rush through Jordan. *She is interested*, Jordan thought. It felt good and seized the moment. It was a new trajectory that he desired but was unprepared. His libido was seeking satisfaction but was not designed to contemplate extenuating circumstances—something a thoughtful mind would ponder at a later time. "Do you have time… want to get a coffee or something?"

"I have time, my class isn't for an hour, that would be

good," Sonya said.

They gathered their things, Jordan a jacket and Sonya the same including her backpack. It was a mindless effort as they left the college and walked about two blocks to a local coffee shop. Upon crossing the street Sonya stumbled slightly and grabbed Jordan's arm as he turned slightly to assist her by placing his right hand on hers as she clutched his upper forearm. They both held on for more than the time required to arrest the incident. The paired touching added to the afternoon's personal intensification.

The small café was intimate and used for poetry and literary readings by the English and Literature Department. A small podium was set aside in a corner of the café. It was dimly lit wood paneled space with natural light only entering through the front glass. There was a coffee and pastry/snack bar with limited table service. Sonya and Jordan took a seat near the front window with Sonya leading the way.

"What do you want?" Jordan asked.

"I like their blueberry scones and a cappuccino."

"Good for you, need those carbs, I'll be right back," Jordan left to place the order and Sonya watched as he did, he glanced back smiling at her while he waited.

Hands full after he received the orders, Sonya got up from her seat to help him. "Let me give you a hand," she said as he handed her the cappuccino and managed the other items. Slowly they returned to the table and settled down facing each other across the small wooden lion paw pedestal table.

"What did you get?" Sonya asked.

"Just a coffee and banana bread. Want some?"

"No, I have enough here, thanks."

The café was empty except for an elderly professor type in the corner, with uncombed hair and unkept beard while wearing a crumpled jacket. He seemed oblivious to everything except the screen on his laptop that had a spreadsheet he was concentrating on. But for the laptop, strewn papers and locale he might have easily been mistaken for a homeless vagrant. Sonya had observed the man while waiting for Jordan to return and asked, "Do you know the guy over there," as she tilted her head without looking in the man's direction.

Jordan furtively glanced in the man's direction and turned to Sonya with a frown, "No, not really, should I?"

"Just thought he might be one of your colleagues."

"Thanks, yeah him and I hang out all the time at the club," Jordan said satirically.

Sonya giggled at Jordan's humor and said, "He's a professor I'm sure, thought you might know him."

"The guy is obviously in the sciences probably math, chemistry or something, he doesn't have time for the superficialities like bathing, haircuts and appearance like us social science types." Sonya reached across the table and playfully slapped his hand as she laughed at Jordan's description.

There was a moment of quiet as they delicately savored their hot drinks with steam emanating out and pinched off pieces of their snacks. Jordan brushed his hand with his napkin after each pinch.

"You know I go out alone a lot. What do you think about that? Is it weird? My friends think so," Sonya offered as a change of subject.

"I don't know, if you are comfortable. Where do you

go…do you meet people after you go out?" Jordan said.

"Yeah, I enjoy myself, usually concerts, clubs…you know."

"I can't believe you're not dating, no boyfriend. I would think most young guys would love to take you out."

"Maybe, but I find most guys don't want to put in the time. They want one thing. Personally, I find older men, mature guys more attractive."

Jordan considered the comment subjectively and thought to himself; *Is she telling me she's ok with our age difference?* You seem older…let me say mature for someone your age. It was one of the reasons I wanted you to work for me. I think age emotionally reflects your life orientation not necessarily its chronology."

"I like that," Sonya said.

"So, tell me what's the most embarrassing thing you've ever done or had done to you?" Jordan asked, probing but treading lightly as they got to know each other.

"What is this some kinda *Truth or Dare*?" Sonya said as she cocked her head with a puzzled look on her face. Before Jordan could respond she sat back in her chair looked upward, touched her brow with four fingers and said smiling. "My god so many I can't think, every day is an embarrassment."

Jordan maintained his posture and looked directly at Sonya saying, "*And.*"

"You mean the fourth-grade play when I fell off the stage and luckily my teacher knew how clumsy I am, maybe not just me, but a lot of the class and placed foam mats at the end of the stage. Still haunts me, it was the highlight of an otherwise dull play...*Wizard of Oz*. Or last week when I accidently sent a text to my baby's daddy, intending to send to my girlfriend and said '*Missing you xoxo*' with emoji hearts and kisses. He texted back talkin' about what took me so long, I had no clue and called to let him know I would never get back with him. So embarrassing!"

"Wow you are a mess, a good one," Jordan said as he chuckled at her matching facial and voice inflections while telling the story.

Sonya suddenly realized the time had quickly passed and said excitedly, "Oh damn, it's almost 2 two o'clock I have class professor, you gonna make me miss it," Sonya emphasized her faux accusation as she got up abruptly and gathered her things.

Jordan stood up to do whatever he could even though there was nothing to do. "Don't want to do that...make you miss class. Thanks, I enjoyed our talk, and call me Jordan outside of class, this is different, we are friends."

The suggestion stunned Sonya and she wistfully said, "Oh okay," not knowing what she was committing to or what it meant. "You owe me, don't think you get away free." Jordan looked uncertain. "Most embarrassing moments," Sonya said

"Ok, yes I owe you," Jordan said as he reached to embrace her--they hugged.

Sonya left the coffee shop to juggle all the demands of an ambitious woman and mother with youthful dreams and energy. Jordan settled down for a moment to consider what had just happened, most of which he had no command, but he knew it felt good and that was good enough for now.

Chapter 14

Jared considered himself lucky to have such a beautiful wife; she was the prettiest girl he had ever dated. They had met years ago when Jared was a presenter at a conference about wealth generation and the benefits of real estate ownership. He was immediately taken by her presence in the small, intimate conference room. She wore a business pantsuit with her hair in a bun; red lipstick gave her a vintage Hollywood look. She was easily the most eye-catching person in the room, of whom the majority happened to be women. After his presentation, she approached him to introduce herself. They decided to exchange business cards, and as she handed the card to him, she said, "Don't take my card if you don't intend to use it."

Blushing a bit and somewhat off balance by her assertiveness, he looked at the card, noticed she worked in Manhattan and said, "Of course, I'll use it. Maybe we can have lunch. I'll call you."

"I'd like that," she responded.

Juanita was a stunning cocoa-brown Bajan beauty. Her eyes were huge and almond shaped, with long lashes and naturally arched eyebrows. Her AncestryDNA.com report would probably show a high percentage from northern Africa, the Middle East, or East India. Jared was instantly intrigued when he met her. In high school, Juanita had been voted prettiest girl in school and had served as prom queen. She had thick sepia-black shoulder-length straightened hair—no weave necessary. She was delicately built with proportionate features, high cheekbones, and a model's height. When she was younger, in her late teens, she'd had a brief career as a video girl and dated several celebrity types and, at one time, a prominent basketball player. She was in her late twenties now, close to thirty, and still as attractive, if not more so. Juanita placed value on her good looks and sex appeal. She used her appeal as a commodity and intuitively used men's reactions to her attractiveness as leverage for her business as a real estate agent. The art of flirting, seduction, and manipulation of the male ego for personal advantage was part of her repertoire. Her personality was easily given to romanticism, idealism, and risk. She was a natural flirt. As a real estate agent, the greatest source of sales was married couples. Juanita sold a package that included more than real estate—particularly to the male clients. One can assume the wives may not have appreciated her sales techniques.

Later that afternoon, Jared was having drinks at the conference hotel's bar with some colleagues and was going over the day's events when he noticed Juanita across the room walking toward the bar. She hadn't noticed him when she entered. Some minutes later, Jared retrieved her business card from his pocket, stepped away from his table, and called her cell.

"Hello," she answered.

"I was just admiring you a few minutes ago and wondered if I could join you for a drink."

"Who is this?" Juanita asked.

"Don't act like you don't know. We spent the afternoon together earlier today."

"What are you talking about?"

"Turn around and look to your right. You'll see a handsome black man admiring you from afar."

Juanita looked over her shoulder, saw him, and smiled.

"You scared the hell outta me. I didn't recognize your voice. I had no clue who you were. Of course, you can join me. Come on over, handsome black man."

"All right, let me excuse myself from my friends, and I'll be right there."

"K."

Jared made haste, politely excused himself from his company, telling the group he was joining a client from the earlier workshop. The group, mostly men, looked at Jared and glanced toward the bar. The collective unspoken reaction was, '*Yeah, we know...go for it man*'. He left and walked to the bar to join Juanita. They spent the rest of the late afternoon into early evening drinking, eating appetizers, and getting to know one another. They shared a lot in common, including an interest in jazz, both classic and smooth. They critically rated movies and Netflix originals and the books they'd read. There was a mutual admiration and uncommon attraction—beauty and brains.

"This has been nice, Jared. I am so glad I came to this conference, but I have to get going. I can't believe it's dark out now," Juanita said after looking at her watch and realizing they had spent three hours together.

"Are you staying in the area? Can I give you a ride to your place?" Jared offered.

"No. I live in Harlem, but my agency is paying for the hotel stay, here . . . small perk. I have some other workshops tomorrow. I'm on a real estate transaction panel in the afternoon, so I need to do some work in my room to prep for that."

"This is it for me. I'm flying out tomorrow afternoon to meet with some clients in DC, then back to Jersey."

"We are neighbors. That's too bad you're leaving," Juanita said.

"Oh? Are you going to miss me?"

"Well, I thought we might spend some more time together, but if you have to leave, I understand," Juanita said as she motioned to the bartender for the tab, they had opened earlier

"I didn't say that," Jared quickly responded, seizing the open invitation. "Plus, my flight isn't until the afternoon."

Juanita grabbed the check the bartender presented, and Jared offered to pay which she refused saying, "I'll expense it, my treat, you can get it next time."

'Presumptuous but correct,' Jared thought.

"Then you can keep me company tonight, but don't distract me too much." Juanita said seductively. She handed the bartender her *AMEX* card and with the same hand tossed the strands of hair hanging over her eye and said with a whisper of allure, "Get the receipt, leave a tip Mr. Baros while I stop by the ladies room to freshen up and we can meet in the lobby. I can show you the spectacular view from my suite."

"Sounds good. I'll meet you out front."

Jared and Juanita spent the evening together. They had a great time laughing and playfully teasing each other. Juanita won the pillow fight but submitted unconditionally to the wrestling match when Jared straddled her and pinned her arms over her head. "You win. You got me. So, what you gonna do with it?" Juanita challenged. Not saying a word, Jared ravished her all night.

The next morning, they had breakfast in bed and good-naturedly showered together, and Jared watched as she dressed and applied her makeup to go downstairs to the conference. She left before him and blew a kiss as she walked out the door. Both lived in New York area and dated for about six months thereafter, when one night at dinner, on Valentine's Day, Jared proposed.

Juanita closed the deal, and a month later, at an intimate wedding of family members and close friends, she became Mrs. Juanita Rhitan-Baros. Jordan and Trina were overjoyed when Juanita and Jared gave birth to a healthy baby girl, Aisha Rachel Baros, some seven months later. They were in the throes of bliss, oblivious to anything other than their moment.

Chapter 15

Sonya again met with Jordan in his office a week or so after their coffee shop dalliance, not counting the classroom lectures. Sonya had texted Jordan since then with cute, playful DMs that Jordan appreciated with an emoji smile and witty response. It was near the end of the semester. They were meeting to finalize everything they had worked on during the preceding months. She had delivered the materials as promised, and he had completed a draft paper and begun the conversion of the document to a PowerPoint presentation. He was pleased with himself and the support of his student research assistant. Their relationship had grown from mentor/mentee to something seeking personal definition. It had started out similar to others, where they would meet to go over things and create a work plan and discuss things such as the project, class assignments, and other students. Jordan always kept his office door open and was careful to maintain a degree of professionalism, always remaining conscious of university policies, especially sexual harassment. He had newly completed a mandatory workshop on the subject. As a result, and given headline news, he examined his behavior more than usual. He was specifically mindful of a point made by one of the panelists in the workshop where she quoted materials from the American Association of University Women's study on sexual harassment that stated:

Colleges and universities foster unusually close relationships between faculty members and students. They encourage a degree of dependence, affection, camaraderie, or collegiality, explicit sharing of values and personal trust that tends to blur the distinction between supervisor and subordinate. It is such blurring of boundaries that may lead to crossing of lines and uncertainty in the nature of the relationship. It is exactly because of this that colleges and universities must remain extremely vigilant about the potential for abuses and violations of boundaries that occur as a result of   unclear roles that may lead to charges of harassment. The institution must therefore ensure the presence of clear policies that speak explicitly to the potential for abuses, while also providing an environment and opportunities to learn and interact while monitoring what may constitute gender-based and other forms of harassment. Linda Gordon Howard, Esq. *The Sexual Harassment Handbook* (2007, p.197)

Jordan googled some additional research to better understand case law regarding sexual harassment in the workplace and on college campuses. Recently, one of the university's professors had been suspended and his retirement, tenure, and career benefits were all in jeopardy. In spite of the professional obligation to comport himself according to the rules, he was intrigued, to say the least, and looked forward to being with Sonya in the privacy of his office after class.

His heightened sensitivity to university policy was without a doubt due to his budding fascination with Sonya. The office meetings were a regular occurrence, and the more time they spent together, the more familiar they became.   The initial bureaucratic protocols were gradually disassembled over time as they consensually moved to an unspoken space of comfort and agreement. Sonya's urges were driven by the idea of natural selection. The professor, from all his students, had selected her, which made her feel special. Professor Baros, a mature older man of intelligence and accomplishment, was indirectly courting her, notwithstanding the risk and social restrictions. His self-assured confidence also expressed protection and security, something Sonya found lacking in her life. *He must know how to take care of and treat a woman*, she thought. And the power of the thought itself was an aphrodisiac.

There was an undefined sexual intimacy in their communications, the personal undoing and sharing as they explored their lives—the commonalities of thoughts. They laughed and talked about cultural and social issues, past relationships, families, and philosophies of life.

For Jordan, it was different, more primordial. Sonya, if described literally, would not sound as striking as she was. She had full lips, Rosario Dawson/Angelina Jolie–like, that were disproportionate to her other facial features. Her eyes, although extremely clear, had no particular hue, and her nose was delicate with limited flesh. Each of her features singularly was attractive but hard to envision if described in response to the question, *"What does she look like?"* However, if an artist were to paint her portrait, it would capture the soft uniqueness of the exquisite combination. The same enthralling reaction happened to everyone who encountered her and had charmed Jordan that first day of class.

Jordan was most enticed not by her facial features, but by her physique. She was of ample proportions, average height of five feet, five inches, about 125 pounds with a relatively small waist pronounced by an above-average hip measurement and prominent buttock. When she walked, she swayed like women of her physique are inclined to do. A juicy hourglass would be the best description—a youthfully ripe beauty that would diminish over time. He had never seen her legs; she always wore stretch skinny leggings or jeans. This day she was wearing an all-black jogging suit and fashionable low-cut black UGG boots. She had discreetly unzipped her jacket and a subtle but obvious showing of cleavage immediately caught Jordan's eye.

"Hi, Sonya. Don't we look nice today," Jordan said as she walked comfortably and unannounced into his office. She sat in her usual chair on the other side of the desk.

"Thanks, Jordan," she responded with swag while unloading her backpack and placing it next to her chair. This was the first time she had referred to him as Jordan since he asked her to do so. "How is the paper going?" she asked.

"I'm finishing up the draft. I'll send you a copy in the next day or two so you can read it and let me know your thoughts."

"Will do. Ugh, I'm so annoyed with the people I'm

working with for this criminal justice group project. Some people are just so irresponsible. We were supposed to have a meeting this morning to go over drafts so we can start to organize and begin putting the final presentation together, and half of them didn't even show up, so me and this other student are the only ones prepared. The shit sucks. Now the rest of us have to get the work done ourselves, or I fail because they didn't do their share. Pisses me off."

"Wow, you are fired up this morning. Can't you and the others go to the professor and explain the problem?"

"Yeah, I should go snitch on those punks. I'm gonna give them one more chance to get it right by Friday, and if they don't, I'll have to work on it all weekend. Can I use your computer? I need to check something on Blackboard."

"Sure. Do you want to switch seats?"

"No, you can stay there. I just need to check one thing really quick."

Jordan stood up and leaned his backside against the credenza behind his desk as Sonya came around, assumed a standing position hunched over the computer's keyboard, and began to enter her login info to the site she needed. She was inches from him, and he looked at her body line from the back of her head with her straight black East Asian partial hair tracks flowing downward. She would primly toss it back from time to time, as it fell over her shoulder while she was typing. Her arched back and her expressive protruding buttocks triggered thoughts and released a lascivious response in Jordan. *I want to fuck her so bad*, he thought. In his younger days, there would have been no question or hesitation. His confidence and urges as a young man instantly dismissed things that he now processed before acting. Plus, he had no reason to hesitate before; his desirability was confirmed by the encouraging responses he received from the women he pursued.

There was over a thirty-year age difference between them. *Why would she be interested in getting involved with an older married man? What would her friends say? Am I grotesque compared to the younger men she could be with or had been with?* His inclinations were more measured now. His previous affairs, infidelity, and behavior trampled on everything he now held dear. He had learned to love and appreciate intimacy. The life he and Trina fought to preserve had blossomed. They had patched together the shattered shards of their marriage, and it had held— withstood the test of time. His two sons, grandchildren, and the love and respect he commanded were supporting evidence. He had always wanted everything that was now his reality. He looked forward to an even better future—to being the patriarch of his family and an example to be admired by future generations. *Why jeopardize and risk the wonder of a fulfilling circle of life by revisiting unfortunate transgressions that were part of a failed distant past?* The erotic urges were measured against his enlightenment—the high one experienced in such a desirable sensual encounter, which would ultimately decline and leave you empty, guilt ridden, and impaired. It was like a sugar high followed by an ensuing downer. Jordan rationally knew what he should do, but passion was an irrational, unpredictable, and powerful force.

Sonya finished and turned to face Jordan. He continued in his relaxed posture, and she did not attempt to move away. He fixated on her gorgeous lips as the thought of kissing her intervened and preempted the previous ruminations. They both sensed the desire. Jordan stood erect as he thought, *I can't do this.* The brief seconds they faced each other seemed like minutes, until Sonya lowered her eyes, turned and walked around to the other side of the desk.

"Let me tend to this other stuff that I have on my plate,

professor," Sonya said, seeking to regain her composure, with imperceptible faint beads of perspiration along her hairline. Possibly feeling Jordan's reluctance, just as she felt his desire minutes ago. The recent comfort in their privacy to call him Jordan, after he had given her liberty to do so receded. Sonya reverted to calling him "professor" having felt the complexity of the mutual urges just moments ago. "Maybe we can go out to dinner like you said after the semester ends," Sonya offered.

"I would like that," he stated. Feeling as if he owed Sonya something, Jordan said, "I apologize if I made you feel uncomfortable just now."

"No need to apologize; you did nothing wrong. It felt good," Sonya responded.

"OK, things can get complicated . . . Hopefully you understand. Thanks for everything," Jordan said, unsure of what to say.

"It was my pleasure; text me if you need me," Sonya said as she briskly, awkwardly and slowly gained composure while preparing to leave.

"OK. I will." Jordan said as he settled into his chair and did not attempt to come from around his desk.

Jordan knew, even if not consciously, that the proposed dinner date would never happen. Sonya and Jordan remained in contact after the school year ended. They texted, followed each other's social media sites, and called occasionally. They shared personal developments without any intimations of relational needs. When the situation allowed, they planned to meet for dinner or lunch, but it never happened. Even when they set a date and time, one would call the other to apologize for not being able to follow through with the commitment. Unspoken thoughts were loud and clear—what might have been would never be. The universe was vast and constantly expanding. The desires that intersected at a particular time were eventually eclipsed and never to intersect again.

Chapter 16

It had been a few days since Wanda returned from Africa. She had taken Imani to her pediatrician and spoken to Rachel, her mother, every day since returning. She was in a rehabilitation facility regarding her speech and right-side motor skills—all of which were affected by the stroke. Wanda was going to the hospital to introduce her mom to her newest grandchild.

Wanda entered the room and saw that her mother was lying in bed napping, as was Imani in Wanda's arms. She quietly placed the baby's bag and her pocketbook on a chair and unwrapped Imani from her pink and green crochet blanket as she approached the side of Rachel's bed. Before she could reach the headboard, Rachel opened her eyes and beamed a smile that covered her entire face.

"Oh my gracious, look at my grandbaby," she said.

"Mom, can you sit up?" Wanda asked.

With strained effort, Rachel sought to better position

herself as Wanda adjusted the automatic bed lift to raise it higher. She handed Imani to her grandma, who cradled the newborn in her arms and looked intently into the now alert Imani's sparkling brownish eyes. Imani returned her grandmother's stare just as intently. Rachel started to sing the lyrics she had sung to all her children at one point in time. Wanda smiled as Rachel recited in melodic lyrics:

> "Put on the skillet, put on the lid
> Mama's gone make us some short'nin' bread
> That ain't all Mama's gonna do
> She gonna make a little coffee, too
> Well, Mama's little baby loves short'nin',
> short'nin'
> Mama's little baby loves short'nin' bread
> Well Mama's little baby loves short'nin',
> short'nin'
> Mama's little baby loves short'nin' bread."

Imani enjoyed it as much as Wanda. "She's smiling," Wanda said.

"Yessum is mommy's little baby," Rachel said in a distinguishable southern black dialect, a rhythmic cadence, still beaming from when she opened her eyes. "She's adorable, Wanda."

"How are you feeling, Mom?" Wanda asked as she leaned in to kiss her on her forehead, thinking to herself, *Mom looks better than I anticipated, thank God.*

"I'm doing fine, love—just a little sore from the bed. They're taking me to rehab during the day. Slowly but surely, I'm gaining my strength," Rachel said in a measured expression.

"You look good. Who did your hair?" Wanda asked, admiring the intricate cornrows. "The nurse said that you'll be coming home soon."

"Oh, thank you, baby. One of the little nurses, a black girl, braided it for me the other day. I hope so. The food is horrible. Can't have any salt or seasoning. I wish you would have snuck me some Lawry's."

"Oh, Mom, you know you can't have that. It's good to see you still have your sense of humor though."

"Hopefully, that will be the last to go. So, tell me, how was the trip?" Imani had dozed off after grandma's singing and was more than content in her grandmother's arms.

"Oh, it was wonderful! We had such a great time and ended it with a beautiful gift from God."

"Oh, that's so good to hear."

"How's your boyfriend, Reynaldo?"

"Reynaldo is fine. He actually wanted me to tell you hi and that he'll be coming by to see you. He had to work today—had patients."

"Tell him hi, and I'll see him when I get home. So how are you doing with the baby and all?" Rachel inquired.

"Everything is fine. It's kind of hectic. Luckily, I'm my own boss, so work stuff is on hold for the moment, but I do love being a mommy."

"You have a beautiful girl, Wanda. Raise her to be as wonderful a daughter and woman as yourself." Rachel felt prideful and admired her daughter's happiness and their shared living joy embodied in Imani. "Hopefully, she'll bring you as much joy as you have me. She is one of a kind—unique but the same—she is us. Let her magic blossom."

Wanda appreciated the expressions from her mother and felt emotions that went deeper than the instant--a lifetime of feelings and thoughts poured forth as she continued to listen. "It is a joy like no other. You will have both the good and the bad, and there will be trying times, but those are the things that keep us going—they allow us to get up when we get knocked down. You have to teach her to deal with it all—the wonderful ideas and magic that are within her. Let her life continue the journey on the road that we all travel, as did our ancestors before us, and in doing so, help her find who she is."

"Mommy, that is so sweet. I will. After all, I had a great teacher," Wanda said with a smile.

"So, this must be your daughter I hear so much about," the nurse, a tall black woman said as she entered the room.

"Yes, it is. This is my Wanda and my new granddaughter, Imani," Rachel said.

"So glad to meet you. Your mother has told me all about you. Congratulations on your daughter. My name is Gladys. Your mother is a wonderful person; we all enjoy her."

"Thank you. Are you the one who did her hair?"

"Yes, that's her. She looks after me," Rachel said before Gladys could answer but, nodded in agreement.

"Well, thank you for looking after Mom."

"No problem at all. You know how we are with our hair," Gladys said with a chuckle. Wanda shook her head in agreement without the need to say more.

"Mrs. Lady, you have an appointment with the physical therapist, so we're going to have to get you up and into the wheelchair. Do you want to go with her, Wanda?"

"I would, but I really have to get the baby home," Wanda said, turning to her mother. "You gonna be OK, Mom? We'll see you in a couple of days. I need to take the baby home now."

"I'm fine, dear. Don't worry about me. Have you talked to Jordan?"

"Yes, he's coming over later today, and he came by the house the other day."

"Good. He's been taking care of me. He's a good boy."

"I'm glad to hear that, Mommy. We'll see you soon," Wanda said as she again kissed her mother's forehead and gently took the sleeping Imani from her arms. She tucked Imani into her blanket as the nurses helped Rachel sit up as they strategically placed the wheelchair on the side of the bed before helping her down and into the chair to go to the physical therapist.

Wanda made her way toward the door while looking back at her mother. Rachel smiled with satisfaction for both her daughter and her grand.

"Thank you for everything, Gladys," Wanda said as she walked out of the hospital room, down the long natural colored corridor and glistening tan linoleum flooring, glancing into rooms filled with the infirm and family members comforting their loved ones.

Chapter 17

They were cuddled together, her backside touching his crotch. The pleasant organic scent of her Aveda hair conditioner traced his nostrils as Chad gently kissed the sensitive nape of her neck, causing goose bumps on her shoulder and upper arms. "That was amazing," he whispered. She didn't respond but turned to give him a look of pleasurable satisfaction that said it all. Repositioning herself and pressing her backside harder against his pelvis, she reached back to grab his buttocks and pull him even more against her plumpness.

"I'm amazed each time we're together. Do you believe in a cosmic force that makes sex better between certain people?" Chad said.

"Am I the best for you? I'm not going to say, 'the best you ever had' 'cause y'all say so whether it's true or not. Plus, you just came. You'll say anything."

"Not true. I'd 'say anything' before I cum, not after, but you really are a beast and the best no doubt. But you know you're taking advantage of an amateur at this."

"Chad, stop. You're lying—as many women as you've had. How many is it?"

"Why do you want to go there? And who's counting? I honestly don't know."

They both settled back as she pulled the sheet partially up her leg just below the curvature of her backside. Chad placed his hand on the indentation between her hip and ass. She felt the warmth of his hand, the security of human touch, and the freshness of Egyptian linen cotton against her skin. Chad knew the liaison was not over as she had previously reached back to press him into her. She was now reaching down to stroke his flaccid dick. It didn't take much, and the soft tender strokes easily prompted a reaction. Chad knew her amorous needs were grand, and he used supplements to enhance his performance. Since drug testing was not required for sex games, he felt justified for both himself and his partner. She had asked him on occasion if he took Viagra because she found his stamina and hard-on to be unbelievable. Chad always denied the question, and he was not exactly lying—it was Levitra, not

Viagra. He thought it was better for his pleasure, and her ego, to think it was solely her sensuality that stirred his amorous desire. She turned and went under the sheet to place him in her mouth and began to cup his balls as she tongued the underside of his penis. He responded and moved to place her underneath to enter her missionary.

"Wait a minute, baby, let me get my toy," she said as she moved to the bedside, reached for her leather Coach backpack, and pulled out a pink pouch.

"You're going to use my little friend, I like that," Chad said.

She returned to her prior position, clicked the button on her vibrator, and placed it on her clitoris as he straddled her, supporting himself with his arms to give her hand space to manipulate the sex toy.

"OK, sweetie. You all right? You want to fuck me while I masturbate?"

Chad entered her vagina as she continued to double play her clit with the toy and his penis. It was unbelievable. She could feel his girth expand as she moaned under the pleasure of the duality. Her wetness and his expansion brought them to the edge of ecstasy. She stopped the sex toy vibration and was completely joined with him. "Take me, you son of a bitch. Fuck me on the edge of this bed like you would fuck a whore." They held each other and plunged together into the synchronized infinity beyond, like pairs figure skaters closing out their routine.

"I'm cumming, baby. Let me pull out and come on your tattoo. Turn over!" Chad had run out of condoms earlier, and no matter how pleasurable, coitus interruptus stepped in to arbitrate the situation.

She did as he asked and turned to feel the wet ooze splash on her lower back where her Chinese sunflower tattoo with its prominent yellow coloring and aqua-blue leaves was. The tattoo represented both energy and passion. He whimpered like a baby to her exhilaration. She laughed—not a humorous laugh, but a fulfilled one. The sex elicited crazy reactions—laughter, crying, sadness, and elation—an indescribable orgasmic cornucopia of emotions.

There was an instant of sedative silence, which they both wished could last forever—unfortunately, her cell phone rang. In agreement with the mood, the ringtone was a soft twinkle and not a jarring rap tone or Beyoncé belting "Put a ring on it!"

"Should I answer that?"

"Do we have a choice? Go ahead."

She reached for the phone, ignoring the prompt as to who the caller was, "Oh, hi. Yes, I'm wrapping up with one of my clients and will pick up Aisha. Yeah, we can figure that out later. There's some ground beef in the fridge, or we can order pizza in. Let's decide when you get home. I have to run. I'll see you later, OK? All right, bye."

Chad heard the entire conversation including his brother's voice on the other end. He heard Jared say, *'I love you'* before they hung up. Most noticeable was Juanita's failure to respond in kind. The mood changed completely. There was a look on Juanita's face that said everything. Chad buried his head in the pillow. The soulless treachery they both felt was a bolt of depravity that was always there and inescapable. It was an affair approaching incestuous dimensions—her husband's brother, his sister-in-law.

"I have to go," Juanita said. "And we have to straighten up in here. I'll put the sheets in the wash and do them tomorrow.

Juanita had access to one of her client's penthouse suites as a managing agent until the place was rented. She and

Chad took full advantage of the situation and rendezvoused as much as two times a week—occasionally more, depending on the time of the month. They were both inexplicably on the same bio-clock and just before her period, which coincided with the full moon's cycle, they both became particularly horny. It is said that female roommates will, after living together, develop the same menstrual cycle. She gathered her wedding ring and sundry items from the night table, placing the ring on her finger— not exactly the one Bey was referring to. She led the way as they left the apartment.

* * *

Juanita was his sister in-law, and Chad initially respected that, even if he harbored a more-than-familial interest in her from the first time they met. Now that he was living with her and Jared, Chad saw her daily, and it triggered some suppressed emotions. All his life, he had been "finding himself" and was approaching thirty. It was easy to strike up conversation and share personal feelings with Juanita. This was exactly what happened. From the beginning, there was playfulness between Chad and Juanita. Everyone, including Jared found it, at most, amusing. Jordan, who tended to have a keener reaction to subtlety than others, noticed the extra attention Juanita gave Chad. She laughed at his jokes more heartily than they deserved, hung on to his words with her eyes when he spoke, and if he left the room, she watched until he disappeared. He noticed but did not process the thoughts as anything untoward. He blocked the unthinkable because to countenance it would be unmanageable and emotionally unfathomable.

Chad was not working, and Juanita's work schedule was flexible. Jared was never home. As a result, they spent more time together than she did with her husband. On a typical day, Juanita would get the kids ready for school and day care. She would return to find Chad preparing coffee and breakfast, or on occasion, they would meet at Starbucks or another coffee shop. The time together served each other's social needs. They enjoyed the companionship and fell into a pattern, looking forward to the time together each day.

Things remained relatively innocent, each tossing out sexual innuendos, flirting, and becoming increasingly touchy-feely over time. He helped her put her coat on and opened doors while touching her waistline or lower back to lead her forward, and in the car or sitting across a table, she would delicately touch his hand or knee while making a point about something of interest. Chad shared his growing interest in Juanita with a friend while masking her identity and the true facts. He wasn't sure, at that point, what was happening, but deep down, he knew, even if he didn't let it surface.

They were out one evening as a threesome; Jared had an extra theater ticket to see *The Color Purple* on Broadway with Jennifer Hudson as the lead actress. The seating arrangement placed Juanita in the middle of the brothers. When Jennifer sang the title song, "Color Purple," with that thunderous voice that shook the theater, Juanita, who had been clandestinely playing footsie with Chad throughout the show, sunk her manicured nails so hard and deep into his arm during the audience's standing ovation to Jennifer's rendition that it made Chad yell out, "Oh my God, girl. Wha' the—?" Everyone assumed his outburst was an uncontrolled exuberant reaction to the vocal athletics he had just witnessed, not realizing the paralyzing pain Juanita had inflicted with her claws. She just smiled, and Jared remained naïvely oblivious.

Another change was evident as Juanita started wearing outfits that were more revealing. "How does this look, Chad? Is it too tight? Make my butt stick out?" she would ask while looking over her shoulder and allowing him to observe her side profile. "Nothing you can do about that," Chad would respond, and she would turn and slowly walk away, feigning embarrassment while giving him a better look at her posterior.

The first time they were together was unplanned. Juanita had just returned from dropping the kids off and was upstairs in her bedroom. Chad went upstairs to look for his phone, which he thought he'd left in one of the kids' rooms. He passed by the master bedroom; the door was wide open. Juanita was in full view, half-undressed. He froze and stared at her magnificence. She immodestly stood there and let him. He entered the bedroom, and she moved toward him and shut the door behind him. They made love on the carpeted bedroom floor. One can conjecture that they thought by doing so, maybe their behavior was less egregious than if they had consummated their sex act in the bed—at least a bargaining chip if and when they got to heaven.

For weeks after their first encounter, they intentionally avoided each other. Juanita didn't come back to the house after taking the kids to school. Chad would leave early and return later in the evening. But this didn't last, and eventually, the artificial wall crumbled. They resumed their earlier patterns, daily texting and planning their schedules to include time together. After the initial sexcapade, they never again had a tryst in the home, but as we now know, Juanita had access to some of the most opulent homes in Essex County. Their luxurious and treacherous love making continued unabated.

Chapter 18

Jordan was in his office one early morning, having a coffee and pastry while scanning the day's headlines when he received a call from Chad.

"Hi, Dad, how you doing?"

"Good, my man, how are you? What's up?"

"Just calling to see if we can talk sometime this week. I have some things I want to run by you."

Jordan was both surprised and elated. He loved the idea that his son was in the area now. He saw more of him than he had in years. But Chad still maintained a personal privacy that was hard to penetrate. His reaching out felt good to Jordan but was also uncharacteristic. "Of course, son. You tell me where and when. If you want, you can come by the house this evening."

"I was hoping we could meet away from the house.

What about Loco's Tacos? I haven't been there in a while and feel like Mexican."

"No problem, son. You want to do it tonight?"

"Yeah, sure, let's do it tonight. How's seven?"

"Seven it is. You wanna tell me what this is about?"

"I'd prefer to do it in person. We'll talk tonight when I see you."

"OK. I'll see you tonight."

"See you later, Dad."

That's curious, Jordan thought, and couldn't imagine what Chad had to tell him. Normally, Trina would give him a heads-up regarding things with the kids since she was more in touch with them than he was. But he couldn't recall anything she'd said recently that would indicate what Chad wanted to talk about. He gathered his textbook and class folder, realizing he'd find out soon enough. There was no need to ponder, and he proceeded to class.

* * *

Jordan arrived at the restaurant before Chad and asked for a corner table in the bar area. The restaurant was sparsely occupied, as Jordan inhaled the tantalizing scents and aromas of dozens of Mexican dishes being prepared. From flavorful street foods like tacos, and burritos to more authentic classical dishes—all with fresh vibrant ingredients. A short, square-shaped Mexican waiter led him to his seat and handed him a menu, placing the other one on the side where Chad would be seated.

"Can I get you something to drink?" he asked in a distinctive Spanish accent.

"Yes, I'd love a margarita, no salt," Jordan replied as he began looking at the menu. Before the waiter returned, Chad entered and approached the table. He was dressed casually in an open jacket, denim jeans, tan boat shoes, and Ralph Lauren plaid fitted shirt. A lean and tall Jordan stood to greet him and flashed a smile of approval at his handsome looking son.

"Hey, boy, how you doing?"

Answering his question with a question, Chad asked," You been here long?"

"No, I just got here a little before seven. I just ordered a margarita. Sit, it's good to see you. You are hard to keep up with."

"Yeah, I know. Since I moved back, I've been really busy. I guess Mom told you that I was by last weekend. You were off playing golf, so I missed you."

"She told me. When are you going to get out there with me? Once you start, you'll love it."

"Man, I wish I had the leisure time that you do. I can't spend five, six hours chasing a little white ball in the grass all day. Plus, last time I tried to play it was torture. I was so terrible. It was embarrassing."

"It's not about that. It's the open space, exercise, and the challenge of it. It's Zen-like; your mind is focused and concentrated on controlling a situation that is uncontrollable and unpredictable. All your problems are on hold for five hours. It's refreshing, if you don't take it too seriously."

"I hear you, and I'm sure I'll get into it eventually, especially if you keep bugging me about it. Jared and I haven't forgotten the lessons we had when we were young. I'll get back out there with you one day."

"I'll be looking forward to that. Have you seen your

Aunt Wanda and your new baby cousin yet?"

"Yeah, I was by Aunt Wanda's a couple of weeks ago. Imani is getting big already. She's cute. It's nice to see Aunt Wanda so happy."

"Yeah, it really is nice. That reminds me—we're going to have everybody over in a couple of weeks for a barbecue, invite the family to celebrate everything. We haven't done that in a while, and your mother really wants to do it. We'll let you know."

The waiter brought Jordan his margarita, chips and salsa and asked Chad what he would like to drink. He ordered a beer.

"You need more time to order, or do you know what you want?" the waiter asked.

"I know; do you, Dad?" Chad said, looking at his father.

"Yeah," Jordan responded, ordering the chicken enchilada dinner. Chad got the shrimp fajitas.

"You've always ordered shrimp fajitas since you were a boy."

"I know. This place always brings back memories, just

like the Italian hot dogs we used to get after my games. We've been coming here for years."

"I know. It's comfortable and nostalgic, and the food has always been the same—so good. So, what's on your mind these days, young man?"

"A lot. I honestly don't know where to begin," Chad haltingly said. Jordan didn't respond and waited for Chad. "Let me start with some good news. I got an advance from a publisher, and my book will be published and released next year, so that's a relief."

"Oh my God, that's great! I am so proud and happy for you, son. That's been a long time coming. I guess coming home was the right move after all. You've worked so hard on this; it's been years. You deserve it."

"Yeah, it's definitely been a challenge, but you've always said perseverance and hard work are the keys to success."

"This is your accomplishment. You should be so proud of yourself. When did you get this news?"

"It's been in the works for some time. It was finalized last Monday. My agent let me know that they're giving me a hundred thousand dollars in advance and fifteen percent royalty on sales after the release. We were trying to get twenty percent. This is more money than I've made my entire life."

"Your mother will be so pleased. I guess you haven't told her?"

"Nope, you're the first person. I wanted to make sure everything was in order before I said anything. There's been so many disappointments that I waited till I signed the contract before I accepted it as true."

Jordan felt personally awarded to know that he was the first Chad had disclosed the good news to. The reward a parent feels from the accomplishments and successes of their children can exceed their personal achievements. This is what Jordan was feeling from Chad's announcement. "You always had it in you. Even as a child, you would write those stories and read them to me and your mother."

"Yeah, I remember, but the thing that stands out the most was when I was a freshman in military school and won a writing contest for my grade."

"Yes, you were so proud, particularly because no one knew you had such talent. Even your English teacher was shocked," Jordan added.

"Remember when she called me on stage, and said I was not one of the usual suspects she thought would win the award. The entire audience laughed and said my name. I loved that moment. But it is not easy; there are stops and starts."

"What do you mean?"

"They call it writer's block, Dad. It happens. Its unexplainable but a very empty feeling. The creative forces and imagination that roll out when I'm productive just disappear. It's like I'm driving and forget where I'm going, and I don't know what it takes to get my bearings."

"Well, you found it. This calls for a toast." Jordan raised his glass, signaling Chad to raise his bottle of beer. They clinked the glass of each. In spite of it all, Jordan could not help but notice the lack of exuberance in Chad's eyes, given such a momentous accomplishment. There was a despondence that did not coincide with the moment. "You don't seem happy. Why are you so somber? You should be celebrating," Jordan inquired to try and understand the disconnect.

He hesitated and averted his eyes away from his father

before answering the question. "There's something else I have to tell you."

"What? Are you all right?" Jordan immediately responded with a slight sense of urgency in his voice.

"This is not easy, but I've been agonizing over it for months. I don't know how to say it other than just to say it . . . I . . . uh . . . had relations with Juanita."

"You've been in a sexual relationship with your brother's wife? Are you kidding me?! Are you insane?" Jordan exclaimed.

Chad fell silent and felt the incredulous stare and saw the frowned brow on his father's forehead. The silence lasted indeterminably. Chad wondered if he had done the right thing disclosing his secret. Jordan was stunned and momentarily speechless as he processed what he had heard.

"I can't believe you. Are you that self-centered and so callous to do that to him—to your family? Your actions affect all of us, our family, but I assume it didn't even enter your mind. Your brother loves you; he admires you . . . has always done so. He took you in. Doesn't that mean anything to you? Doesn't that concern you? Does he know about this?"

"No, I moved out some time ago. He doesn't know."

"He must never find out, Chad. It will destroy him. No one is to know; this ends here, you hear me? What about Juanita? What has she said?"

"We haven't talked since I left, but I ended it about a month ago."

"What is to stop her from telling Jared?"

"I don't think she will. They have their own problems. It has been bad for some time. She is in therapy; he stays away a lot—working, traveling. They sleep in separate bedrooms."

"That's no reason for you to do what you did. He gave you a place to stay, and this is what you do?"

The emotions triggered by Chad's disclosure transcended everything and evoked other deep-seated feelings. Jordan felt no hesitation or reservation about those affections. He spoke of the hurt he and Trina patiently endured as Chad had distanced himself from the family. The questions they asked themselves as parents and whether they had unconsciously failed to love and protect him.

"We allowed you, as painful as it was, out of love and respect, to be your own man. It hurt not to hear from you; it was as if you despised us—me, really—and I could never figure out what I did to make you resent me so much. Your mother consoled me, at times telling me you were going through your journey, to be patient. We instilled the right values in you. I didn't accept your rejection. I have always committed myself, my energy and thoughts to you and your brother. I wish I had had the support and love I gave you boys. Every day I ask myself, 'How can I do better by my family?' You haven't reciprocated. Why?"

"Dad, I have no answers for you. I struggled early on—didn't finish school, didn't particularly know what I wanted to do. It was hard to face you and Mom. Y'all sent me to military school when I was thirteen. I let myself down, but more importantly, I knew I let you down. I know how much you have done for me, and for that I am truly grateful. I wanted so much to please you from the time I was little. I always fell short; it was easier just to stay away."

Jordan heard Chad but didn't listen. It was noise that seemed secondary to the more pressing issue of familial deceitfulness. "You must promise me that you will never repeat this to anyone. This is a secret that you take to your grave. You are going to deal with this the rest of your life. How you choose to live with this, I have no idea. The shame and humiliation every time you see your brother, nieces, and nephew will haunt you forever. I'm not a therapist, but I have lived life fully, and there are things in my life that I deeply regret and still live with. I am still healing and so will you. All you can do is try and become a better man . . . a better person." Jordan didn't want to go down the same path he did with Jared and felt the situations were different but felt compelled to inform Chad of his own failings and times in life he was not proud. He ended his excoriation with a testament for the future.

"I knew I loved you, your mother, our family, and willed the strength to persevere for the wonder of it all. Everything I now have, is the realization of that love— especially your mother's support. You will have to decide for yourself the man you are and want to be."

"I know. Even with the book deal, I feel like shit. It is all percolating inside, and it hurts. But not just that; it's the entirety—constant struggle and tests, failures, hopelessness, getting back up."

"I don't know what your book is about, but I assume

that it must express some of what you have gone through the last years," Jordan said.

"It's strange that you would say that. It's so amazing; I've been more productive these last months than I've ever been. The shame and trauma I was feeling was being expressed in my writing. My work is a call for help, a catharsis and confession—search for salvation. My demons and goodness have been in a battle for my soul. I know I'm responsible for my actions, and regardless of what I've done, I am a good person, but the other side is so strong and calculating."

Like an attorney making an impassioned closing to a jury in a case involving life or liberty, Jordan stated that he didn't have as much time as his son on this earth. And the family, its legacy for future generations, was very important to him. "I hope that you find someone and have children of your own. I hope and pray for that for you. We all prosper as individuals and family if our lives are not about selfish narcissist objectives, but shared values and purpose. I need you to understand that. All this philosophical talk is good, but there is a reality that we all must face in life. Your existence is only worthwhile to the extent that it is part of something larger than yourself. You must face that reality head on, not deflect or avoid. I am here for you, but this is your life, and you are making a mess of it and everyone else's. I am so disappointed in you."

"I intend to change," Chad responded.

There was not much more to say. Jordan felt emotionally exhausted. Chad needed his father but was numb—he had no clear thoughts; in fact, he felt worse than he had before he told his father.

Before they had finished their meals and drinks, Jordan stood up, put cash on the table for the bill the waiter had earlier delivered, and said, "I'll see you, son. This ends here, you understand?"

Chad followed his father out and while standing outside on the sidewalk said, "I know, what you mean, I will never talk about this to anyone, please don't tell Mom. Thanks, Dad. I'm sorry for everything."

Jordan nodded; he didn't embrace his son as usual and quickly turned to walk away.

Chapter 19

Rachel was readmitted to the hospital months after her previous stay. It was a cloudy morning, overcast with a wind chill that was ten degrees below the recorded temperature. Jordan was making coffee; he had not slept well the night before. His cell phone rang—he could see it was Wanda calling and picked up right away. "I can't understand you, Wanda; slow down," Jordan said.

Wanda repeated over her sobbing, "She's gone, Jordan! She's gone!"

Jordan had emotionally reconciled the unavoidable-- death is an inevitable part of life. He knew before she repeated her statement and was not traumatized—but stunned, frozen in place. In spite of hearing the news, his immediate reaction was not to focus on his feelings, but to console his sister. "She was a good person, our mother. She loved us both," he said, in an effort to console her pain.

"I was headed over there this morning, and the day nurse called and told me that she found Mom in bed, not breathing," Wanda said.

"She passed in her sleep?" Jordan asked.

"The nurse said she thought at first she was sleeping, but she noticed a facial expression that was unusual, so she looked closer. She could see Mom smiling, but she wasn't breathing, and her lips were gray."

"She died peacefully, no pain. That is good; have some solace in the fact that she didn't suffer."

"They pronounced her dead early this morning," Wanda said, still whimpering as she spoke.

There is no right way to deal with the death of a loved one, let alone a parent, and each individual handles the shock and grief differently. Wanda needed comfort and to be surrounded by others—family, friends, and well-wishers. Jordan internalized his grief and isolated himself from everyone, retreating to personal space, introspection, and solitude in his house. Trina allowed him to grieve, offering consoling words of support and listening when Jordan wanted to talk, but she didn't push him.

***

Wanda spent the second night after her mom's passing having dinner with Romeo and another friend named Nia. They met at an Indian restaurant in Manhattan on Lexington, near 37th Street. She wanted to be with her closest friends. The solemnity of the evening was apparent, and her friends hugged her warmly when she came to their table.

"How are you, sweetie?" Romeo asked as Wanda prepared to sit down.

"Not good. I'm still processing the fact that my mother is gone, and I will never get to talk to her again."

"I am so sorry for your loss, Wanda," Nia said warmly.

"I wrote the obituary this morning and relived so much. It's so hard to describe the process. At one point I felt that she hadn't died. It was as if she was right there with me, telling me what to write."

"I hear that's actually common," Romeo sympathetically said. "When my mother died, I had visions of her when I was out shopping or anywhere and thought I would see her coming toward me. It's the spirit. It's a part of you and will always be there."

"I'm emotionally distraught. Jordan needs to be busy to get through this, so he's handling all the preparations for the funeral. I don't know how he does it. I have no energy. I break down every day and just cry." She started crying after finishing her thought.

Nia and Romeo sat quietly letting the collective motions do the speaking before saying, "Let it out Wanda. It will be all right."

"This is so embarrassing. I'm sorry."

"Don't you dare," Romeo said. "I'll beat your ass, and I'm not going to say, 'Be strong.' If you need to cry, girl, you just cry."

Nia was shocked at the 'beat your ass' comment and told Romeo, "You shut up."

Wanda giggled at the comment and Nia's fussing with Romeo. His comment and the way he said it was so outrageously inappropriate, she had to laugh.

"I didn't mean it like that; you know what I'm saying. Just do you, Wanda. You're allowed to," Romeo said.

"Let me give you a hug with your crazy self," Wanda said. "I don't think I've laughed in days." Romeo went around the table and hugged Wanda. Nia got up from her chair, too, and the three friends all embraced.

Nia softly held Wanda's hand as Romeo stepped back. "I know it's hard to believe right now, but you'll be fine," she said. "We are all different, but there are stages to the grief that we all go through, especially when we lose a parent. You will go through an extended period of sadness, a longing for the past when she was alive, and maybe regret that you didn't spend as much time with her as you should have."

"Thank you, Nia, I appreciate it," Wanda said.

"So when you feel like that, or when you feel alone and need some love, just call me. We'll get through this together. Remember when I lost my dad some time ago, and you were there for me? I will never forget that, and I got you now," Nia continued to express her sympathy.

Romeo spoke additional words of sympathy. "You will regain strength; you have to. And as you do, you'll begin to experience your mother in a new way. And as time passes, you will envision and accept a spiritual relationship. It will give you the comfort you need. We are there with you, and we all will heal."

Nia's and Romeo's words were comforting, appropriate, and needed. They finished eating and spent some time catching up on things, including some gossip about mutual acquaintances. Wanda threatened to end her friendship with Romeo if he didn't visit more often and told him his goddaughter, Imani, missed him. He promised to do so but deflected by saying she hadn't thanked him for the baby clothes he recently sent. Wanda left in better spirits and appreciated the consoling words her friends provided. Nia and Romeo promised to attend the wake and funeral in a few days.

Chapter 20

The ride to the church seemed unusually long, and countless thoughts raced through his mind. Jordan had long contemplated his mother's ultimate fate. He hadn't prepared a written eulogy but had, over the last few months, formed one in his mind. The last time he saw her, he was wrought with pain. The sight of her wasting body; yellowish complexion; thin, frail hands; and sunken eyes was too much for him to bear. He now sought to organize a lifetime of emotional and physical experiences they shared—the treasure chest. He recalled a vision that had worried him years ago when he was at his lowest point. He had imagined being at rest in a cathedral-domed church, lying in a coffin, with a black choir all dressed in white, singing gospel hymns. Bouquets of multicolored flowers were all around, the floral scent pervading the air and uplifting the celestial spirits of those attending. Today, as he entered the church, that vision was crystallized. It was not him in the coffin, as he had dreamed, but his mother, and all their family, friends, and acquaintances were assembled.

All stood as Jordan, the family patriarch, entered from the back of the church, walking down the aisle with Trina. Wanda and Reynaldo followed them, carrying Imani, with Chad and Jared, holding Aisha's and Sean's hands, behind them. In honor of Rachel's life, a blessed communion of happiness and legacy was assembled.

* * *

The solemnity of the moment was upon Jordan, and he felt his mother's spirit as he gathered the strength to approach the pulpit to present to the congregation. He had entertained a myriad of thoughts and feelings all week. *Who was she? Who am I as her son? What was it that she wanted for me...our family?* The thoughts and regrets she expressed near the end had told Jordan that she was questioning whether or not she was worthy of God's exaltation.

Rachel's death caused Jordan to be self-examining, introspective; prompting him to be a more complete man— to use his incompleteness every day as motivation to be a better husband, father, and person in general. He recalled a theory he had learned in college; it postulates that our life's journey is motivated by the satisfaction of needs. The theorist expressed those needs as lower-level survival ones, such as food, shelter, and security. Satisfaction of those things is necessary, but not an end in itself. The theory goes on to describe higher-level needs, such as family, community, friends, intimacy, love, and ego—such as self-esteem and distinction. Once lower-level needs are met, we climb the hierarchy of satisfaction. The theory further states that the highest attainable need is self-actualization. Self-actualization requires uncommon qualities such as selflessness, empathy, humility, integrity, and optimism. Only a small segment of us strive for and attain self-actualization. It's a pyramid of life.

Jordan began his mother's eulogy after greeting all who were assembled: "I remember Mom at our last family Christmas dinner. She had recently been hospitalized, and we told her that she shouldn't push herself. But as we all know, Mom was stubborn and would say, 'Ain't no little high blood pressure gonna stop me from takin' care of my family.' She prepared our last family meal as she always did on Christmas. It was our tradition, and she demanded that we share the holiday together, no matter where we might be. Like homing pigeons far and near, we made the journey to our Mecca . . . our deliverance.

Jordan paused briefly and scanned the congregation before proceeding.

"Mom was a modest woman and was never disposed to excess. Her meals and our time together were like the matriarch in the movie *Soul Food*. There is a tradition in black families—and among poor folks of all cultures—where food is an offering of love and respect. In spite of it all, from slavery to discrimination in modern times, food is sustenance. It is a gift of nurture, care . . . love.

"She raised Wanda and me, and before that, as the eldest daughter, she raised and buried her younger siblings, Uncle Ralph and Aunt Helen. She sat at the head of the table that last Christmas together. There were Cornish hens, turkey, cranberry sauce, mac and cheese, mushroom pudding, cornbread, wild rice, gravy, collards, and homemade rolls. Before the blessing, she asked for our attention, and the dining room table became silent. She told us how much she loved each of us and said that we were the branches of her tree. She acknowledged each of our achievements, the growth of our family, and the shared values. She spoke of the precious gifts—her children and grandchildren. It was a solemn and measured speech that was heartfelt and experiential.

"Today, I appreciate her words even more because I realize, unlike what I thought once before, one does not have to be a historical figure, celebrity, or legend to self-actualize in life. It is your heart and soul that will determine your level of satisfaction in the hierarchy of life. She was not Martin Luther King, Mandela, or Harriet Tubman. She was an unassertive woman who dedicated and sacrificed for the well-being of her progeny. She gave to her husband, her community, to Wanda and me, and the youngest among us—baby Imani—the love and nurturing that only special beings can. She self-actualized through the gift of love that everyone assembled here has experienced when in her presence. Without a doubt, she set a standard for all of us. It is our light at the end of the tree-lined road. In her name and spirit, I implore each of you to take risks and celebrate whenever you can, because life is short, tenuous, and amazingly awesome."

He again paused momentarily, and with a handkerchief, he patted his tear-stained eyes and wiped his brow. Chad and Jared looked straight ahead, expressionless but for their somber, downturned mouths. Trina sobbed silently with her handkerchief in hand, the grandkids' anime eyes were bigger and rounder than usual, and the entire assemblage was mournfully silent. Before Jordan resumed, he looked directly into Wanda's tear-soaked eyes. There was a momentary unison and soothing of the three souls: Rachel, Wanda, and Jordan. Regaining his composure, Jordan concluded by saying, "Bless you, Mom, as you will continue to whisper to us about love, forgiveness, and consolation. Thank you for the gift of life, and may you rest in peace as we carry on here on Earth."

After Jordan's eulogy and the minister's salutations, the coffin was closed, and the pallbearers carried her body to the waiting hearse. Jordan walked down the aisle followed by his family, acknowledging other family members, friends, and well-wishers as he left. Rachel's body was laid in the hearse, and the funeral procession left the church. Jordan and his family rode behind the hearse in a black limousine to the burial site, followed by the procession of mourners in their vehicles.

Trina held Jordan's hand the entire route. Rachel's hearse and the lead limousines were draped with purple funeral flags from the funeral parlor. The other vehicles, headlights illuminated, were led by a police escort. Traffic laws were suspended as the vehicles made their journey. Jordan took note of the respect accorded his mother as cars on the opposite side of the thoroughfare yielded to show their respect for the deceased. After a brief ceremony at the graveside, Rachel was lowered into the ground. Sean, Aisha, and Imani, at Trina and Wanda's urging, each tossed a single red rose into the plot. Everyone returned to the church for repast.

* * *

As one might imagine, the Baroses were emotionally spent; however, the thoughts and prayers of respect, consolation, and warmth were graciously appreciated. Jordan was unexpectedly caught off guard when a woman dressed in black with a fabulous black shawl approached him. She was a handsome woman of middle age he hadn't seen in years. With her was a young girl of teenage years. It was Stacy Watson—Maria Velez's best friend.

"I am so sorry for your loss," she said as she extended her hand to Jordan.

At that moment, Jordan grabbed her hand and pulled her close to hug and kiss her on the cheek. "Thank you for coming, Stacey."

"It's been ages, and I heard about your mother's passing and wanted to offer my condolences."

"Thank you so much. How have you been, and who is this pretty young lady with you?" Jordan said.

"This is Jamella. Jamella, this is Mr. Baros," Stacey said as Jordan extended his hand to the young girl, and she reciprocated.

"Such a pretty girl. She's got your eyes. My God, has it been that long? How have you been?"

"Doing fine, still living and working in New York—out in Westchester—happily married and raising my daughter."

"That's so nice."

"Jamella, honey, go get Mommy something to drink—water or something, it doesn't matter."

"So nice to meet you," Jordan said to the girl as she left to do as her mother had asked.

"I was waiting for the right moment to approach you and felt a little uncomfortable with your family and all . . . your wife. I think back and feel as if I should apologize somehow. And who would have thought . . .? I called Reynaldo after he posted your mother's death on his Facebook page."

"Stacey, no apology is necessary. That was years ago. We have all moved on. Isn't it crazy—Reynaldo, Maria's ex, is with my sister? He's cool. We both avoid the obvious—too embarrassing. It's better that way. This world is unpredictably crazy. Speaking of moving on, how is Maria? Do you stay in touch?"

"You know Reynaldo and I went to college together, right?" Stacey said.

"No, I didn't know that."

"We did, if you can believe that. And yes, Maria and I stay in touch. She moved to the West Coast. Still single, last we spoke. She was working with a PR firm, had a setback, but that was some time ago."

"I heard. Reynaldo—Rey—told me she had an incident with a beauty product she was promoting."

"Yeah, you know her and that hair. She was devastated. Still is. Wears a wig, suffered severe burns to the scalp and hair loss. It upsets me to think about it. Her mother passed years ago, and after her divorce from Reynaldo, she left the area." Stacey also knew that Maria, like her mother, who had died of breast cancer, had recently been diagnosed with the same genetic mutation. The gene dramatically increased

the chance of contracting potentially fatal breast
cancer. Some women with such diagnoses opted for double
mastectomies and reconstructive surgery. Stacey felt it
inappropriate to communicate Maria's private medical
information to Jordan and didn't.

"That's sad. I wish her the best. Well, thank you for
coming, and I'm so glad to see you are doing well. You
look good."

"It is good to see you after all this time. Let me go see
Reynaldo, and maybe I'll see you later. My best
regards...sympathies to you and your lovely family."

Jordan felt a tinge of sorrow and a pinch of déjà vu. He
remembered the times and the youthful energy when they
were so familiar and their mutual connection to Maria
Velez. How amazing the way time reorders, adjusts,
dismisses, and heals. It's an extraordinary phenomenon. A
living organism that absorbs and regenerates in perpetuity.
The conversation with Stacey, back to the past, was a
distant memory, and things that at the time had seemed
eternal and so significant had wilted like plants without
water or light. He surmised that if you lived long enough,
all things eventually assumed their proper place, and there
became a rational order to the universe.

Epilogue

Last time **Jordan and Trina** were spotted, they were relaxing in chaise lounges on the deck of a cruise ship somewhere in the Caribbean. Both were sipping margaritas and listening to cool jazz on Spotify while reading books. Jordan would occasionally pull down his sunglasses to the tip of his nose to peek at one of the many string-bikini-clad young women as they sauntered by. Trina was aware of his indiscretion but said nothing, as she was equally guilty of admiring the abs on the taut young men at poolside.

Wanda and Reynaldo are happily living together raising Imani in Brooklyn Heights, New York, in the same building as Romeo. She had her first birthday and is healthy and happy. There are no immediate plans to move to South Africa. Jordan advised Wanda to get a palimony agreement, which she did, and Reynaldo had no problem signing it. There are no immediate plans to marry.

Jared and Juanita divorced and share custody of Aisha and Sean.

Chad's book was published, and he is writing his second novel, hoping for a movie or TV deal. He remains single but is dating. He took part of his royalties and set up a 529 college fund for Aisha, Sean, and Imani. Chad has never disclosed the secret to anyone. He and Jordan will take it to their graves.

Acknowledgements

Thank you, family. To Michelle: I apologize when I was staring into space and you would ask, "What is wrong with you?" and I would say, "Nothing." Truth is, I was writing a book in my mind. Ryan, Kyle, Hemilyn, Sean, Myles and Leila for the cocoon of love and comfort now and forever. Special thanks to my super editor and counselor, Rita Pira for her valuable services and as we liked to say, 'let's make this *#%&* sing'. My extraordinary cousin Mark Clark II for the wonderful artwork and cover design. To my friends who were so supportive of my first novel *Other Side* and especially the North Jersey Links who I hope to call upon for this book.